"Please don't mention what we discussed earlier."

Her sister's invitation to dinner to Jean-Luc de Sauvignet filled Jilly with apprehension. What if he let slip what she'd told him?

"Jilly, you've told me about your physical problems—you don't by any chance have a personality disorder, as well, do you?" he murmured. There was a glint of mockery in his disconcertingly blue eyes.

"You're really enjoying this, aren't you?" she accused angrily. "I foolishly confided in you in the erroneous belief that you were a doctor. And not being a particularly good judge of character, I didn't suspect what a warped sense of humor you possess!"

"But at least I possess a sense of humor. See you later, *chérie*," his softly laughing voice called after her as she stormed away.

KATE PROCTOR is a British writer who has lived most of her adult life abroad. Now divorced, she lives near London with her two grown-up daughters and her cat Wellington. She is a qualified French teacher, but at present devotes all of her time to writing.

Books by Kate Proctor

HARLEQUIN PRESENTS
1195—SWEET CAPTIVITY

KATE PROCTOR

wild enchantment

Harlequin Books

TORONTO • NEW YORK • LONDON
AMSTERDAM • PARIS • SYDNEY • HAMBURG
STOCKHOLM • ATHENS • TOKYO • MILAN

Harlequin Presents first edition March 1990
ISBN 0-373-11253-X

Original hardcover edition published in 1989
by Mills & Boon Limited

CHAPTER ONE

'I KNOW you didn't miss me, so don't pretend you did, Charlie Miles.' Jilly Marshall picked another morsel of fish from the bowl beside her on the floor and offered it to the huge tabby cat sprawled next to her.

Having accepted the titbit, Charlie returned to eyeing the slight, golden-haired figure sitting cross-legged beside him with his customary bored disdain.

'Don't think I'm going to sit here hand-feeding you,' chuckled Jilly, promptly doing precisely that. 'And in case you were about to ask—I didn't have a pleasant time at the hospital; in fact, I had a rotten time of it. I'm sick and tired of being prodded and yanked about by doctors...Charlie, you're a lazy so and so,' she laughed, as the cat butted his head against her hand in demand for more. 'Your ma's hardly going to thank me for spoiling you even more rotten than you already are.'

Both cat and girl pricked their ears at the sudden shrill summons of the doorbell.

Jilly leapt to her feet, hastily wiping her fishy fingers on her jeans and almost tumbling over the cat darting between her legs to rush ahead of her. It was as the two of them reached the front door that Jilly cast a cautious look in the tabby's direction and spotted an almost maliciously anticipatory gleam in his huge topaz eyes. It wasn't that Charlie *always* maimed unexpected callers, she reasoned optimistically, then decided to opt for safety.

Stretching out her right leg, she held the cat at bay with her foot, then opened the door.

It wasn't the sharply rebuking nip Charlie inflicted on her, as she opened the door, that caused the problem—and anyway, it was her right ankle that received the punishment—but one moment her left leg, now taking all her weight, was a solid prop beneath her, and the next it had all the solidity of under-set jelly.

As the door swung open Jilly found herself swinging with it before ending up sprawled on her back.

'Are you all right?'

The voice asking that question was deep and masculine and contained the merest hint of surprise.

Jilly tried looking up to see who had spoken and found herself gazing straight into the face of the plainly enraged cat.

'Get off, Charlie,' she begged, reaching out to heave him from her chest where he stood, hackles raised, glaring threateningly.

Just as she was having second thoughts as to the wisdom of her intended action, Charlie let out a growl of outrage as he was picked up and dumped unceremoniously on the floor beside her. Without Charlie to impede her view, Jilly tried looking up once more, only to find the late-afternoon sun right in her line of vision. Those parts of it not blotted out by the tall, broad-shouldered figure of a man were shining straight into her eyes.

'Do you need a hand up?'

Without waiting for her reply, two hands grasped her by the upper arms and drew her to her feet.

Before she could even begin to voice her thanks, Jilly gave a yelp of surprise as her body began tilting forwards till it met that of the man before her, then began sliding slowly down the length of him.

And there was quite a lot of him to slide down, she noted inconsequentially in the split second before she was grasped once more, this time quite painfully, by the arms, and hauled upright.

'Entertaining though this undoubtedly must be for the neighbours, don't you think we should see about getting you on to a chair?'

There was a sudden movement, then Jilly felt herself swung aloft in a pair of strong arms and carried down the hall.

As she clung to the lapels of the pale stone-coloured suit jacket, the pungent aroma of Charlie's fish wafted to her nostrils.

'Put me down, I'll be OK,' she exclaimed in agitation as her eyes, not daring to look at the fine cloth of the jacket for fear of what they might find, trained themselves on the chin of the face above hers.

'Let's get you sitting down,' muttered the man, twisting to manoeuvre the chair and practically suffocating Jilly as her face became trapped between his shoulder and chin.

'I really am sorry about this,' she managed to gasp, feeling her eyes must be widening noticeably as she got her first glimpse of the perfect stranger. Perfect being the operative word, she thought with a mental gulp. Tall, dark and every other cliché imaginable—and then some!

'I just don't know what happened,' she croaked eventually. 'I'm terribly sorry...'

'The point is, how do you feel?' he asked, his eyes suddenly alighting on Charlie whom he impatiently nudged out of the way with the aid of an elegantly shod foot.

'I'm perfectly all right, thank you,' muttered Jilly, her hackles beginning to rise. How dared he treat poor Charlie like that? Then she felt a small stab of disappointment as the cat contented himself with no more than a malevolent glare in the direction of the man's ankles before stalking haughtily from the room.

'Would you mind telling me who you are?' asked Jilly quietly, her gratitude now on the wane. It would have served him right if Charlie had bitten him—come to think of it, it was amazing he hadn't.

'How remiss of me—my name's Jean-Luc de Sauvignet...'

'You're Lady Lou's grandson?' squeaked Jilly. 'You can't be!'

''If, by Lady Lou, you refer to your neighbour the Dowager Marchioness—yes, I am her grandson,' he murmured with a small mocking bow.

'But you speak English...and you're too old...'

'Too old for what? I'm thirty.' There was open amusement in the eyes that slowly swept her slim body. 'At a guess—roughly twice your age.'

'If you were twice my age, you'd be forty-four,' snapped Jilly, aware of how appallingly juvenile her words sounded, even as she uttered them. She was sick and tired of people misjudging her age, but being mistaken for fifteen she found positively insulting. And she was also having considerable difficulty believing he could possibly be Lady Louise's grandson...the Dowager Marchioness, as he had so pompously pointed out. Of all her grandchildren, the French one was unquestionably her favourite—yet this man had practically kicked Charlie! 'I got the impression you were a lot younger,' she muttered suspiciously.

'It's one of my grandmother's quirks—the fonder she is of you, the more she speaks of you as though you were a child. You, I take it, are Jilly—the budding ballerina.'

Jilly nodded, distracted from her somewhat hostile thoughts by a stab of anxiety at the mere mention of the word ballerina.

'The twenty-two-year-old who looks all of fifteen,' he added mockingly.

'Very amusing,' she retorted sharply, annoyed with herself for rising to so transparent a bait.

Much as she adored the slightly eccentric Lady Louise, she was beginning to suspect the grandson left much to be desired, despite his extravagantly good looks.

'I suppose you want the spare key,' she muttered ungraciously, then found her attempt to rise halted by the firm hand placed on her shoulder.

'That can wait,' he stated brusquely, his quite startlingly blue eyes narrowing suddenly. 'My grandmother mentioned your having injured yourself some time ago—has that anything to do with your prostrating yourself at my feet just now?'

Jilly opened her mouth to reply, then closed it abruptly, frowning as she gazed down at her denim-clad legs. She was sitting here, getting uptight about someone again taking her for younger than she was . . . when the fact was that something—probably catastrophic—had happened to her body only moments ago and had scarcely registered in her mind.

'I've no idea what happened just now,' she muttered, trying to retrace the incident in her mind. 'I didn't feel any pain . . . my leg just seemed to disappear from under me.'

'Shouldn't you use a stick, or something—till you're over the injury?'

Jilly glanced up at him, her expression guarded. 'I am over the injury—I'm just waiting to be given the all clear to get back into training.' That was one way of putting it, she added grimly to herself.

'You plan doing your training while flat on your back, is that it?' he asked drily, as Jilly braced herself to stand.

'Do you mind not doing that?' she exclaimed sharply, as he automatically positioned his tall, athletic body as though preparing for her inevitable fall. 'You're making me nervous!'

'I repeat, the only training you'd be capable of would be from flat on your back,' he drawled, not moving. 'Now, stand up.'

'I remember now,' stated Jilly, her blue eyes hostile as she remained seated. 'I tripped over Charlie.'

'OK—you tripped over the cat—so, stand up.'

'I don't wish to stand up, Monsieur de Sauvignet, I'm perfectly comfortable where I am,' she retorted, inwardly cringing at the childish petulance in her tone.

'If you wish to be formal, the correct title is doctor—but Jean-Luc will do.'

Jilly felt her cheeks stain with embarrassment. She'd had no idea he was a doctor. Suddenly she was seeing his questions not as the overbearing and personal probings they had first seemed, but as professionally pertinent.

Not intending to make a bigger fool of herself than she already had, she stood up.

Once more the pungent aroma of Charlie's lunch was in her nostrils as her hands clung to the lapels of the immaculately tailored jacket.

'Perhaps you should sit down again,' he suggested, the heavy raven blackness of his hair falling untidily across his forehead as his face lowered towards hers in concern.

Jilly shook her head, gritting her teeth as a searing pain began travelling from her hip down the length of her leg.

'I've got the feeling back in my leg,' she managed, through still clenched teeth.

'And not a particularly good feeling,' he observed, with what she took to be clinical detachment.

Though she released her frantic hold on his lapels, she was grateful for the light support of his hands on her arms as she took a couple of tentative steps. When those steps grew firmer, he released his hold, watching in silence as she walked twice round the large oval dining-table.

'If only your grandmother were here!' she blurted out, a note of panic in her voice. 'She's the only person I can really talk to!'

'But you live here with your sister and brother-in-law—surely you can speak to them,' stated Jean-Luc de Sauvignet, his eyes shrewd and watchful as they followed her.

'Yes...no...oh, heck, this is no welcome for you! Would you like a cup of tea—coffee, perhaps? Then I'll get you that key.'

Her every movement betraying her inner agitation, Jilly made her way towards the kitchen section of the large, open-plan room. She was brought to a sudden halt by a firm hand on her arm.

'I'll make some tea—you sit down. And, as there's no one else available, I suggest you talk to me—you obviously have to talk to someone.'

Jilly obediently moved back towards the chair and sat down, watching in silence as he filled the kettle and plugged it in.

There was an easy, almost graceful fluidity in his movements which she found slightly surprising, given his well above average height and the impression of compact solidity in the lean athleticism of his body.

He was right, though. If she didn't talk to someone soon, she felt something would snap in her before long— but to this man?

'The tea's in the container to your left, and the cups in the cupboard above you to your right,' she told him, realising glumly that his type was probably the last she would ever have chosen to confide in. Not because he was a stranger, nor a foreigner either, not that one would ever have guessed, there being no perceivable trace of French in his pleasantly musical, though decidedly upper class accent. It was more to do with his looks—that devastating brand of attractiveness which, whether in a male or female, always tended to leave her feeling somehow gauche and more than a trifle inadequate.

'Do you take milk?' he enquired.

'Yes—it's in the fridge... over there,' muttered Jilly, fascinated and slightly envious of the complete lack of self-consciousness with which this stranger could stroll into unfamiliar surroundings and make himself so at home. It was almost as though he were the host and she the visitor, she thought enviously, as he placed two cups of tea on the table and took a seat beside her.

The man was a doctor, urged a small, insistent voice within her, and he had offered her an ear... by telling him, she might even be able to get a little information out of him... and in her present state of uncertainty, any crumb of information would be welcome.

'Do you happen to know of a good dry cleaner?' he asked out of the blue. 'There seems to be a strong aroma of fish emanating from me,' he added, the slight quirk of his lips in an otherwise deadpan face making Jilly squirm inwardly with embarrassment.

'There are plenty around here,' she replied stiffly, convinced it wasn't just her vivid imagination making her certain she was being well and truly made fun of.

'Good.' He raised the cup to his lips, his vivid blue eyes coolly clinical as they surveyed her over the rim. 'Tell me, do you always look so apprehensive—or is it just me?' he murmured.

He could patronise her all he damn well liked, she thought furiously, but she intended picking his supercilious brain as much as she could.

'No, it's just that it frightened me—my leg going from under me like that—it's never happened before.'

'When did you have this injury?'

'Over three months ago—this particular one,' she muttered, her hands fidgeting with her cup. 'I tend to be accident-prone.'

'Accident- or injury-prone? There is a difference.'

'Injury,' she sighed, accepting his probing as that of a competent doctor. 'My left knee and ankle have always been weak spots.' She hesitated, frowning. 'At least, I'd always thought they were the problem; you see, I had trouble with turn-out right from the start.'

'Turn-out?' he echoed, plainly not familiar with the term.

'You obviously know nothing about ballet,' she murmured with a small smile. 'If my leg's up to it, I'll show you—it's easier than explaining.' She rose, relieved to find her left leg feeling virtually normal.

Standing before him, she placed her heels together, rotating her thighs till her feet achieved an angle of one hundred and eighty degrees.

'That's turn-out,' she told him, then laughed at the expression of disbelief on his face.

'You seem to be turning the entire leg out from the hip down,' he exclaimed, aghast.

'That's the whole point—if the thigh bone isn't properly turned in its socket, all you do is twist out your knee and ankle, putting a damaging strain on both.'

'And you don't consider you're putting any strain on your legs the way you're standing now?' he demanded, an expression approaching disgust on his handsome features. 'God almighty, it's completely unnatural!'

'It's the way every ballet dancer stands,' she explained, surprised not so much by his ignorance as by his obvious distaste for something that was the basis of her art. 'It's something that develops with training, but with more ease for some than for others.'

'And you've never found it that easy?' he asked, the question more in the rise of the elegant black arches of his brows than in the tone of his words.

'Not particularly,' she muttered, unwilling to go into what were often the physical agonies entailed in dancing—she had a strong feeling his attitude would fall far short of sympathy.

'If your problem isn't your knee and ankle, what is it?' he asked.

Jilly shrugged, an almost diffident movement of her slight shoulders. 'When this particular injury took so long to right itself, the ballet company decided it was time to let the experts give me a going over.'

'And?'

'And nothing,' she sighed, with a tinge of apprehension. 'I saw them for the third time today.' Her slim figure shifted uneasily on the chair. 'I've been X-rayed and put on weird machines, measured and prodded and yanked about in every conceivable manner. They tend to act almost as though I weren't there. Today I got up the nerve to ask what they were doing . . . what they were looking for. They said they couldn't tell me anything till they had the results of the tests—which wouldn't necessarily show anything specific.'

'Which hardly reassured you,' he murmured. 'More tea?'

Jilly shook her head. 'I'm clueless when it comes to medical jargon,' she blurted out. 'But, from what little I've gathered, they seem to think it's my hip that's causing my problems . . . the one part of my leg I've never had any trouble with . . . until what happened when you arrived.' She took a breath, steeling herself. 'The pain I had, when the feeling returned to my leg, was centred in my hip . . . look, I know it's probably against all medical ethics,' she pleaded. 'But if you've any idea what they suspect the problem is, I'd be most grateful if you'd tell me.' Her heart sank as she saw a frown flitting across his brow. 'I promise I shan't go to pieces, no matter how serious it is . . . it's just the uncertainty's making me so nervous. I haven't been able to mention it to Linda— my sister—because I know how she'd worry . . .' Her words petered to a halt as she heard his groan of protest.

'Jilly, if you're under the impression my doctorate's in medicine, I'm afraid you're mistaken.'

'You mean to tell me you're not a doctor?' she exclaimed, aghast, leaping to her feet.

'Not of medicine.'

'But you must have realised what I thought! I'd hardly prattle on the way I did to a complete stranger, not unless I felt I had good reason to!'

'I was under the impression you were in need of a sympathetic ear,' he murmured, with a dismissive shrug she found galling.

'You thought wrong,' she retorted coldly, humiliation and consternation flooding through her as she picked up their cups.

'You have to admit it . . . you needed to tell someone,' he pointed out, upsetting her further with the hint of boredom in his tone.

'Not a total stranger,' she retorted, marching to the sink and almost hurling the cups and saucers into it.

As she swung round to face him once more, she gave a strangled gasp as pain once more shot down her leg.

'I'm sorry there's been this misunderstanding,' he stated, his expression bordering on apprehension as he rose and approached her. 'Don't you think you should take the weight off that leg?'

With a helpless glare in his direction, Jilly limped back to her chair. 'It would be better if you forgot everything I've said,' she suggested stiltedly.

'Hardly realistic,' he observed, returning to the chair beside hers and sitting down. 'Besides, I gather you'd have confided in my grandmother, so why not regard me as her substitute?'

'I'm glad you find this so amusing,' she retorted, stung by the undisguised mockery in his drawling tone. 'Strange though it may seem, I have a living to earn and dancing happens to be my livelihood.' She hesitated, recoiling from the realisation that antagonising him might not be the wisest of moves. 'If you so much as mention this to my sister, I'll . . . I'll never forgive you!' She felt herself cringe with embarrassment at the childishness of her words.

'For heaven's sake, stop sounding so paranoid,' he exclaimed impatiently. 'Your secret's safe with me—though I'm puzzled.'

'Really?' she snapped, the futile wish that she could erase the past hour from her life flitting through her mind.

'I can understand your not wishing to worry your sister—at a pinch—but, with my grandmother not around, surely you could have confided in a friend . . . or brother-in-law?'

'I don't know David, my brother-in-law, all that well—not that he's not an exceptionally nice man—besides, he's in America on business at the moment.'

'What do you mean, you don't know him that well—you live in his house, don't you?' he asked, puzzled.

'Only since my accident,' she muttered uncomfortably, remembering Linda and David's offer of a home with them when they had married three years earlier—and their patient demolition of her every argument against moving in with them three months ago. 'Anyway, I'm sure David would only have told Linda if I'd confided in him.'

'And your friends?'

'My friends are all dancers,' she exclaimed impatiently. 'The last people to speculate with over possible injuries.'

'Hardly worth calling friends,' he drawled scathingly.

'They live with the constant threat of injury hanging over them, not that you'd understand what that means,' she retorted angrily, then lapsed into a morose silence. All she wanted was for him to leave. 'I'll get you the key,' she stated abruptly as he made no effort to continue the conversation.

'This is crazy!' he exploded, getting to his feet in the instant Jilly did. 'There are a few strings I could try pulling . . . to help get this sorted out.'

'It's very kind of you,' murmured Jilly, guilt stabbing through her at his concern. 'I'm sure the doctors will get me sorted out eventually, so pulling strings could hardly help.'

'But I could arrange for the company to send you to other specialists . . .'

'What company?' asked Jilly, regarding him with total bewilderment.

'The company for which you dance,' he exclaimed. 'My grandmother obviously saw no reason to mention the fact that I've recently been saddled with administering my grandfather's Arts trust . . . hell, the amount of money I've signed over to them in the past couple of years, the least they can do is listen if I ask for you to see other specialists . . .'

'Hold on . . . just one moment,' croaked Jilly, sinking back on to the chair she had so recently leapt from. 'You seem to know nothing about ballet, yet you're telling me you more or less finance the company I dance for?'

'That and several others—not to mention opera companies. My grandfather left a considerable fortune to the Arts . . . surely you know how fond my grandmother is of . . .'

'Yes!' exclaimed Jilly, her mind reeling. 'I just hadn't . . . I just hadn't realised exactly . . .' Her words petered to a miserable halt. She just hadn't realised exactly who it was she was confiding in about her physical inadequacies!

'There's nothing to realise—I merely follow the advice of experts and sign over the money. But, if you're not happy with the doctors you're seeing...'

'I *am* happy with them,' protested Jilly, his words tempering the panic of her confusion slightly. 'These things take time, I know. And I also tend to exaggerate the least little niggle...I think I have a very low pain-threshold.' She rose, her face brightening suddenly. 'Come to think of it, the way they were yanking me around today, it's a wonder I haven't seized up completely!' she exclaimed, relief flooding the delicate oval of her features and bringing them the glow of beauty. 'A good long soak in a bath is probably all I need to rid me of these twinges. And that's precisely what they are—twinges!'

CHAPTER TWO

'JILLY, I'm home! Jilly?'

'Coming!' called Jilly, running a comb through the glossy cloud of amber-gold hair that tumbled heavily to her shoulders, then giving a start of surprise at her own reflection in the dressing-table mirror. 'It's amazing what a bath and some plain talking to oneself can do,' she chuckled, addressing the cat grooming his snowy-white bib with noisy concentration as he lay by her feet. She had been in a state verging on panic—now her common sense had taken over. 'Now I almost look as good as I feel!'

And her leg felt perfectly normal, too, she thought in relief as she sped down the stairs to greet her sister. 'Linda, I'd no idea of the time—I meant to have the kettle on.' She gave her sister a quick hug, before racing over to grab the kettle.

'My, you're full of beans,' murmured Linda, hope now sparkling in the rich emerald-green of her eyes. 'Good news at the clinic?'

'Just the usual,' replied Jilly vaguely, concentrating on filling the kettle and praying Linda wouldn't choose today to take up questioning her specifically, as she had on occasions recently.

'Jilly, I know you don't like talking about it . . . you're not worried you might lose your role in *Swan Lake*, are you?' Linda took a seat, her eyes saddening at the sight of her sister's visibly tensing back. 'Rehearsals don't start for ages yet—and even if you weren't fit by then, there will be other opportunities. You've begun to make a name for yourself...once you're over this...'

'It's only the thought of Carla Simpson being offered the role in my place that would miff me,' butted in Jilly, hating herself for the deception. Telling Linda as little as possible until the true extent of her injury had been decided meant she was unable to mention her conversation with Jean-Luc de Sauvignet...and the strong reservations she still had, despite her recent optimism.

'Poor Jilly,' murmured Linda, coming to her side and taking the kettle from her.

'Stop encouraging me to wallow,' chided Jilly, retrieving the kettle and giving her sister a gentle push. 'You sit down and put your feet up—I'm making this. You've been looking whacked recently—so no arguing!'

With a rueful chuckle, Linda returned to her seat.

'Linda, you know how bitchy I always am about poor Carla,' grinned Jilly suddenly, an impish beauty lighting her face.

'I take it she's the one with her eye on Justin,' chuckled Linda.

'The very one,' laughed Jilly. 'She's welcome to him as a boyfriend—but I'd not give him up as a partner without a fight.'

'Jilly, you're twenty-two!' protested Linda with a groaning laugh. 'Don't you think it's about time you got your priorities right?'

'Not really,' grinned Jilly. 'Like most beautiful-looking men—my brother-in-law being a rare exception—Justin isn't exactly over-burdened with personality, but he happens to be just what I need as a dancing partner.'

'Your theories on men baffle me,' laughed Linda, opening her briefcase and rummaging in it.

'I've merely observed that the really dishy-looking ones tend to rely on their looks to do the talking,' murmured Jilly, pouring the tea. 'Your having married an exception doesn't alter that fact.'

'How about your observations on this,' chuckled Linda, extracting a glossy photograph and slapping it on the table.

'Wow!' gulped Jilly, glancing at the full-length photograph of a man, naked save for a pair of skimpy black briefs. 'According to my theory, this specimen should have absolutely no personality at all! Who on earth is he?'

'Nobody,' chuckled Linda. 'It's a sort of compilation photograph. You remember those vast sums I told you we'd forked out for market research?'

'To find the perfect man?' groaned Jilly sceptically. The world of advertising, in which Linda was a junior executive in an up and coming company, often struck her as being far more steeped in fantasy than her own world of ballet ever could be.

'Perfect by advertising standards,' corrected Linda. 'Don't you understand, this man could make us? According to the research psychologists, he could sell cat food to people who didn't possess a cat!'

'Don't you mean women?' teased Jilly, letting out a yelp as Charlie sprang on to her lap and casually lacerated her thighs as he sought a position of comfort.

'You're wrong,' declared Linda. 'Apparently this one comes over as a man's man to males while at the same time devastating the females. It's all been minutely researched.'

Flashing her sister a look of pure scepticism, Jilly picked up the picture and examined it. This time she examined it minutely, her eyes suddenly widening in disbelief while laughter began bubbling weakly inside her.

'You're supposed to drool, not giggle,' complained Linda with a rueful laugh.

Trying to keep her face straight, Jilly cast her mind back. Had she drooled, she wondered, when she had, give or take a few minor facial details, clapped eyes on what could have been this man's twin? The problems with her leg had distracted her somewhat, she reminded herself, then gazed innocently at her sister.

'By the way, Lady Lou's grandson's arrived.'

'Heavens, I'd forgotten he was due!' groaned Linda. 'What on earth possessed her to ask her grandson over while she's away...a young French boy, who probably doesn't speak a word of English!'

'He speaks English,' managed Jilly, having difficulty keeping her face straight.

'Of course he does,' exclaimed Linda. 'I remember her mentioning he was educated at Harrow—or perhaps it was Eton. What's he like? I suppose he speaks English better than we do...Jilly, I take it you've invited the poor child round to supper?'

'No, I haven't!' exclaimed Jilly. 'And that poor child is thirty!' she added with a giggle. 'What's more...' She gave a strangled gasp as laughter overcame her.

'Jilly, for heaven's sake, what's the matter with you?' demanded Linda impatiently. 'You could at least have asked him round. I'll go and do so now.' She hesitated, her gaze apprehensive as it alighted on Charlie. 'God, I hope that wretched cat doesn't take a dislike to him,' she added anxiously, watching him nervously from the corner of her eye.

'That wretched cat?' exclaimed Jilly indignantly, hoisting Charlie up in her arms and burying her face in his silky fur.

'Jilly, if he bites you, don't expect any sympathy from me. And it's not hygienic the way you're always kissing him—sometimes I get the feeling you're as besotted with him as Lady Louise is, if that's actually possible,' she added with a sigh.

'It's a blessing you're such a confident lad, Charlie,' murmured Jilly placatingly. 'Otherwise you'd end up with an inferiority complex,' she added with a grin, returning the cat to the floor as her sister shook her head in disbelief.

Her expression returning to one of scepticism, she looked at the picture again, this time experiencing a niggling sensation of alarm as she gazed down at the almost familiar face.

'What would you do if you found him?' she murmured.

'My nut!' exclaimed Linda. 'Our agency would be made for eternity if we got the likes of that signed up.'

Jilly returned the photograph to the table. 'The likes of that happens to have moved in next door—not that you'd ever get him signed up...'

'Where?' demanded Linda. 'At the Morrisons?'

'No—Lady Lou's grandson...it's practically him to a tee.'

'Very funny,' exclaimed Linda, flashing her a hostile look. 'I wish you wouldn't always take the mickey out of my job...'

'Linda, love, I swear I'm not!' protested Jilly. 'It could almost be him...go round and have a look, if you don't believe me!'

'I can hardly go round and gawp at the boy—I mean, man...'

'I'm sure you'll stop thinking of him as a child once you see him,' laughed Jilly. 'If you plan having him round for supper—why not go and ask him?' she added innocently.

In the end it was Jilly who had gone round to invite him, her state of mind decidedly wary.

'What will we be eating?' he demanded, in reply to what she had considered to be a perfectly civil invitation.

'Steak, I believe,' she retorted, her expressive eyes telling him in no uncertain terms what she thought of his lack of manners in asking.

'I was merely asking in order to know what wine to bring,' he drawled, having taken in every last nuance in her look, and obviously relishing the opportunity of proving her mistaken.

Jilly felt her jaw clench. 'I hope you remember not to mention what we discussed earlier.'

'So do I,' he murmured, the blue eyes mocking unashamedly.

'Look, if there's any likelihood of your blurting it out, I'd rather you just didn't come round,' she exclaimed apprehensively, realising that if anything came from those almost smirking lips, it certainly wouldn't be by accident.

'If you think I'm about to blurt—just call me *grand-mère*, that should do the trick,' he murmured innocently. 'Tell me, did the bath work the wonders you were hoping for?'

'Yes,' she replied, with an evenness she far from felt. 'There's absolutely nothing wrong with my leg any more.' She turned to step over the flowerbed, her shortcut next door, when a hand halted her by lightly taking up a handful of her hair.

'Jilly, you've told me about your physical problems—you don't by any chance have a personality disorder as well, do you?' he murmured, with what many might have regarded as sympathy had they not taken the trouble to look for the glint of mockery in those disconcertingly blue eyes.

'You're really enjoying this, aren't you?' she accused, angrily tugging free her hair. 'I foolishly confided in you in the erroneous belief that you were a doctor. Not being a particularly good judge of character, I could hardly have been expected to realise what a warped sense of humour you possess!'

'But at least I possess a sense of humour. See you later, *chérie*,' his softly laughing voice called after her as she stormed from him.

She glanced down as she felt a furry warmth against her legs and was horrified to find Charlie's outline blurred by tears of pure rage.

'Why on earth did your ma run off and abandon us?' she exclaimed, incautiously hoisting her unpredictable friend in to her arms and hugging him tightly. 'One thing's for sure—that pervert's not looking after you, don't you worry!'

'Jilly? God, you're not still drooling over that cat!' exclaimed Linda from the doorway. 'Did you ask him?'

'Yes, I asked him,' snapped Jilly, releasing Charlie as tolerence of her reckless hugging gave way to a warning growl. 'And you're welcome to him . . . the man's a positive pain!'

'Jilly, what happened?' demanded Linda, her eyes anxious as her furious-faced sister stormed off and into the large kitchen-cum-dining room. 'Jilly!' she exclaimed, rushing after her.

'It's just that he's . . .' Jilly's words came to an abrupt halt—in her anger she had almost blurted out too much. 'It's probably just me,' she finished lamely. 'I took an instant dislike to him. Would you believe it, he actually referred to Lady Lou as the Dowager Marchioness? And he also kicked Charlie—well, he practically kicked him.'

'Sit down, I'll make us a fresh pot of tea,' sighed Linda wearily, picking up the kettle and filling it. 'Jilly, I've been wanting to talk to you for some time . . . but you've been so tense recently . . . Jilly, will you for God's sake leave that cat alone?' she exclaimed impatiently as her sister stooped to stroke Charlie, who had sprawled himself at her feet. 'I'm sorry, love,' she sighed, as Jilly looked at her in alarm. 'It's just that I said nothing when you came to live here and immediately struck up your strange friendship with Lady Louise—even though David and I saw practically nothing of you. But you're becoming almost obsessive about Charlie . . . it's almost as though you're using him as her substitute now she's away.'

'What's strange about my friendship with her?' asked Jilly guardedly.

Linda sighed as she plugged in the kettle. 'Jilly, I'm not criticising your relationship with her.' She hesitated, then moved to Jilly's side. 'To be honest, I was probably a little jealous of it at the start . . . I'd hoped you and I would have a chance to get to know one another better . . .'

'We're sisters,' whispered Jilly, an unaccountable guilt niggling in the corners of her mind. 'Of course we're close.'

'There's no of course about it,' murmured Linda, reaching out and stroking Jilly's cheek in a gesture that was almost maternal. 'You always were such a...a secretive little thing; not that the five-year gap between us helped much.' She hesitated, her struggle to find the right words noticeable. 'When Mum and Dad split up...and you were packed off to ballet school...'

'I wasn't packed off,' denied Jilly miserably. 'I wanted to go.'

'But ten was so young...in my heart of hearts I agreed with Dad,' said Linda sadly. 'You seemed little more than a baby.'

Jilly felt herself tense as she watched the slow, sad shake of her sister's head—this was no topic she wished to discuss.

'But I suppose it was all worth it,' stated Linda briskly, her slim shoulder lifting. 'The name Jilly Marshall has certainly begun to mean something in the world of ballet.'

'Yes, accident-prone, according to the ballet-master,' responded Jilly nervously. The conversation had switched, but to a topic just as unacceptable to her as the first.

'You know what I mean,' chided Linda gently, taking one of her hands. 'But it worried me that this latest injury might be getting you down...such a long period of virtual inactivity.' There was a tentativeness in the eyes that met Jilly's. 'Which is why, in a way, I stopped resenting your unusual closeness to Lady Louise. I suppose I felt you'd someone to confide in, even though I'd have preferred you to have chosen me.'

'All I need is time,' blurted out Jilly, racked with guilt. 'Linda, I know I probably haven't shown it...but it's years since I've felt as happy as I've been since coming to live with you and David.'

'And if he hadn't almost physically removed you from those ghastly digs you were in, you'd never have come,' sighed Linda. 'Jilly, why?'

'I suppose the ballet school became home after Mum and Dad split up. I just got out of the way of a proper family life...then, when Dad died...for a long time I couldn't bear to be near anyone who reminded me of him...and you reminded me. But I missed you so much!' She gave Linda a sudden, fierce hug.

'I wish he'd been around to see you making a name for yourself,' said Linda huskily. 'Despite your denials, I think he was never fully convinced Mum hadn't pushed you into ballet.'

'I've just realised what it is about Lady Lou...she has that same, almost devastating directness Dad often had. You always know exactly where you stand with them.'

'Which is what usually sends the neighbours scuttling away in terror from her,' chuckled Linda. 'But I know exactly what you mean.'

'I know it sounds contradictory,' reflected Jilly. 'But Dad could be very devious at times.'

Linda nodded, a mixture of sadness and humour in her expression.

'I'm pretty sure Lady Lou's the same... It wouldn't surprise me if she deliberately took off for Jamaica so that you and I could have a chance to get to know one another properly.'

'I think you're being a little fanciful, love,' murmured Linda, smiling indulgently.

'But the trip came right out of the blue,' insisted Jilly. 'Do you know her connections with Jamaica?'

Linda shook her head.

'She and Henry Miles honeymooned there. They used to return every two or three years . . . Henry died on their last visit, six years ago, and he's buried there.'

'So it's perfectly understandable that she'd still go back.'

Jilly shook her head. 'I know she wants to be buried there with him when she dies . . . but I somehow got the impression she'd never return there alive.'

'Obviously your impression was wrong,' declared Linda briskly. 'Come to think of it, she probably felt more able to go knowing you'd be around to keep an eye on Charlie—I think she's run out of catteries prepared to put up with him,' she added with a chuckle.

Jilly nodded, smiling as she gave her sister another fierce hug. 'Linda, I don't deserve a sister as understanding as you. I *am* obsessive about Charlie . . . it's just I'm terrified something might happen to him while she's away!'

'Let's get this tea made . . . and prepare for the battle of supper ahead,' she chuckled.'

'It won't be a battle,' promised Jilly, hesitating. Her talk with her sister awakened a strong need to confide—if only partially. 'He administers a trust fund Henry set up for the Arts,' she began, and immediately wished she hadn't as she saw the puzzlement on Linda's face. 'Apparently this trust finances all the major productions of the company I dance with.'

Linda continued to look at her blankly.

'I'd just got back from a session at the hospital when he appeared!' stated Jilly, desperation creeping into her tone.

'So?'

'So...Lady Lou had told him I'm a dancer...probably even that I'm dancing one of the major roles in the *Swan Lake* production!'

'Jilly...I'm sorry, I seem to be missing the point...'

'The point is...Linda, I was hobbling around!' Her eyes widened in hurt indignation as her sister burst out laughing.

'Oh, Jilly, sometimes I really wonder about you!' choked Linda. 'You have visions of him cutting off all aid to the company just because you've had an accident—is that it?'

'Of course not!' exclaimed Jilly impatiently. 'But there's nothing to stop him deciding I'd be...a risk in the role.' She had said far too much, she thought agitatedly, bitterly regretting having raised the subject.

'Jilly, I'm pretty certain financial administrators merely dish out money—they have no artistic say!' Linda responded soothingly. 'They don't go rampaging around the place hiring and firing!'

'You're right,' sighed Jilly, smiling sheepishly. Jean-Luc de Sauvignet had said pretty much the same himself. 'It just threw me when he told me.' Linda's wholly spontaneous reaction had removed the last of her lingering doubts. 'Anyway, I promise to be on my best behaviour this evening,' she murmured contritely. 'In fact, I'll even aid and abet you in trying to get him signed up.' She giggled at the thought. 'I wasn't exaggerating about his resemblance to that picture, you know.'

'We'll see,' chuckled Linda, though her look was sceptical as she poured the tea.

'Oh, you'll see, all right,' laughed Jilly, feeling good as she leaned back and inspected her sister. With that striking blend of dark auburn hair and vivid emerald eyes set in the creamy flawlessness of an almost perfectly oval face, there were few women with a beauty to match Linda's, she decided admiringly. 'Just bat your eyes at him a few times,' she teased. 'You'll probably have him eating out of your hand... if he fell hard enough, who knows, you might actually lure him into a contract!'

'Still convinced I'm the swan and you're the ugly duckling, aren't you?' murmured Linda with a small, disbelieving shake of her head. 'Jilly, haven't you looked in a mirror recently?'

'Until this injury, I was spending eighty per cent of my life in front of a mirror,' countered Jilly. 'You know, one of the most disconcerting things about dancing in front of an audience is the absence of the practice-mirror—I still find myself mentally conjuring it up when I'm on stage.'

'That's not what I mean, as you well know,' chuckled Linda. 'And if you're right about our temporary neighbour...' She rolled her eyes then pulled a droll face. 'Anyway, I thought I'd do salad with the steak...'

'No steak for me,' protested Jilly.

'And that's another thing I've been meaning to bring up, my girl! You barely eat anything—it's not healthy.'

'Now we're back to the mirrors,' laughed Jilly. 'And in them, I can spot ounces, never mind the pounds!'

For Linda's sake she was going to make an effort, Jilly reminded herself as those cool blue eyes dragged them-selves from her sister for an instant and held hers in a moment of mocking challenge.

Not that Linda was being much help, she thought ir-ritably; she was practically drooling over the wretched man, and had been for the entire time since his arrival.

Her eyes softened as they rested on Linda's lovely, animated face. Linda couldn't honestly believe there was the even remotest hope he would be interested in her professional aspirations where he was concerned, she thought anxiously... or could she? For a start, his connections were far too exalted. However much his grandmother might ridicule her titles, her own family had royal connections. And her marriage to 'Henry Miles', as she invariably referred to her adored late husband, had only become acceptable in the eyes of her exalted family once Henry had acceded to his father's marquessate. With that sort of aristocratic blood knocking around in his supercilious body, Jean-Luc de Sauvignet was hardly a likely candidate for the role of male model. But if Linda thought it worth a try... she gave a pleased start as Charlie strolled into the room and up to her, as though offering himself as a topic of conversation.

'You haven't been introduced to Charlie,' she announced, picking up the cat and deciding she would give the Frenchman one more chance. 'Come along, Charlie, meet Dr Jean-Luc de Sauvignet, your ma's... Lady Louise's grandson.'

'I think we can dispense with the introductions to that brute,' snapped the Frenchman. 'Even my grandmother would draw the line at that.'

'But you'll be looking after him,' hissed Jilly through clenched teeth, her good intentions—her vow never to leave Charlie in his care—forgotten as she advanced on the seated man, studiously ignoring her sister's frantically pleading look. 'So, it would pay you to get to know him.'

'Would it, now?' drawled Jean-Luc, getting to his feet as Linda rose.

'I think it's about time I cooked the steaks,' intercepted Linda, flashing Jilly a warning look. 'How do you like yours, Jean-Luc?'

'If you like, I'll supervise,' he murmured, his smile dazzling. 'Then I can't accuse you of ruining it.'

Seething with indignation, Jilly listened to their almost flirtatious banter as she put together the salad, then gave a groan of frustration as she heard him quibble over the size of her steak. She had only agreed to have a small portion when Linda had pointed out their guest was bound to think he was depriving her.

'If I'd wanted more, there's plenty in the fridge—it's just that I have to be very careful what I eat,' she told him.

'I'm sorry—I didn't realise you were unwell,' he murmured. Jilly flashed him a scowling look as his teasing eyes candidly skimmed her slim body.

'Dancers have to be careful about their weight,' she explained, slamming the salad bowl down on the table.

His eyes were wide with exaggerated disbelief as they took their seats.

'From a purely aesthetic point of view, I'd say you could do with at least another stone on you,' he remarked drily.

For Linda's sake, she was on her best behaviour, Jilly reminded herself, biting back an angry retort and flashing her already tensing sister a look of reassurance.

'That remark tells me two things about you.' She had actually managed to sound almost friendly.

'Really?' drawled the man, his attention plainly less on her than on the wine he was studiously sampling.

Jilly felt her back go rigid. Even Linda must see she was going out of her way to be pleasant. Whereas he...the elements of social tact had obviously been omitted from his expensive education, she told herself angrily.

She felt her teeth clamping in irritation as she watched the small frown of dissatisfaction furrow his brow as he swallowed the wine. He brought the damn stuff, so what was he complaining about? One thing she couldn't stand was people who went through all those phoney wine-tasting rituals.

As these decidedly uncharitable thoughts flitted through her seething mind, the dark fan of his lashes lifted, and suddenly his gaze caught hers. His momentary hesitation confirmed, beyond doubt, that he had spotted the hostility she was unable to mask in her eyes. Then he smiled across the table at her, a megawatt smile that immediately filled her with guilty confusion.

'It hasn't travelled too well, I'm afraid...the wine.' He poured some into their glasses. 'You'll find it now merely good, instead of superb. I'm sorry, Jilly—what are these two things you've discerned about me?'

His glance was enquiring and totally lacking the mockery Jilly had expected. Disconcerted, she picked up her glass and took a gulp. The wine tasted great, she decided—then she forced a smile to her lips, conscious of the effort it took.

'Well, firstly you're no balletomane—they always go for line and seem to prefer women dancers verging on skeletal. And secondly, you're no dancer yourself—the men complain loudly about every extra pound they have to lift.'

'Right on both counts,' he murmured. There was open mockery in his glance as he raised his glass casually in her direction before turning his attention to Linda. 'I feel safe in assuming you're no dancer,' he murmured, his eyes almost flirtatious in their appreciation.

'What a tactful way of telling me I'm overweight,' laughed Linda, with the total ease of one confident in

the perfect proportions of her slim, yet appealingly cur-
vaceous body.

She laughed again as Jean-Luc de Sauvignet held up
his hands in theatrical denial.

They were both at it, thought Jilly with a conflicting
mixture of discomfort and envy, conscious that this was
one of those gentle social arts at which she herself was
completely useless. As far as she could remember, it had
always come easily to Linda, she thought, and found
herself hastily stifling the somewhat pious observation
that her sister was now a happily married woman. Not
only would Linda have behaved in exactly the same
manner had David been present—he would not have felt
in the least threatened.

'David takes a very keen interest in my work,' Linda
was saying in reply to a question Jilly's wandering
thoughts had missed. 'He's in international banking and
seems to find the contrast of advertising quite
fascinating.'

Jilly took another sip of her wine, wondering if it
would be now that Linda would take the plunge and
mention the subject which must be uppermost on her
mind.

'Oh—no more for me!' she exclaimed, as Jean-Luc
began refilling her glass.

'Are you never allowed to let your hair down?' he
murmured, confusing her by allowing those strangely
cool eyes of his to linger on the ponytail into which she
had scraped back her hair.

'Apart from administrating your grandfather's trust,
you haven't said what you do for a living,' blurted out
Jilly, wondering what on earth could have possessed her
as she picked up her glass and sipped more of the wine,
her eyes catching his slight shrug.

It was this indefinably Gallic lift of his shoulders that reminded her quite forcefully that this was unquestionably a Frenchman, however much the educated fluency of his English might indicate to the contrary.

'Do? The word implies a definable activity.'

Jilly found his obvious amusement, as he uttered the words, irritating. His manner verged on being gallingly patronising.

'My grandmother's convinced I'm a layabout— perhaps she's right.'

'But your doctorate,' probed Linda, plainly not feeling in the least patronised. 'What's it in?'

'Abstract harmonic analysis,' he murmured, his eyes slightly hooded as they regarded her.

'Is that something to do with music?' she asked, intrigued.

He shook his head, his face expressionless.

'Computers?'

This time he gave an exaggerated shudder of distaste before once again shaking his head.

'Why can't you just accept the fact that he's a layabout?' murmured Jilly cattily, refusing to indulge in guessing games for his entertainment. 'I believe that's still regarded as a perfectly honourable calling among the monied aristocracy.'

'And you're right!' His laughter was soft, slightly husky, and it was tinged with quite genuine delight. 'My grandmother forgot to tell me her little friend studied with the Bolshoi.'

'You obviously don't know your own grandmother too well,' retorted Jilly hotly. 'Her views are every bit as ... as socialist as mine—more so, in fact.'

'Actually, my grandmother and I belong to a mutual admiration society,' he drawled, deliberately goading. 'I happen to be the apple of her eye.'

'Strange that she's barely mentioned you,' snapped Jilly. 'And, if you're that close, how is it you don't even know Charlie?'

'I've known that creature for all six of his bloodthirsty years. Charlie and I mutually settled for a relationship based on total indifference by the time he was a few months old.'

'How on earth could your grandmother have entrusted him to your care, then?' demanded Jilly indignantly.

'She wouldn't dream of it,' he chuckled, raising his glass to his lips. 'Charlie's entirely your problem—or hadn't you realised that?'

'Come on, Jilly, be honest,' chided Linda. 'Lady Louise didn't have to ask—she knew you'd never have spoken to her again had she entrusted her precious Charlie Miles to someone else.'

Jilly shrugged. Any denial would have been an outright lie.

'But you'll have to feed him at night and in the mornings,' she informed the smirking Frenchman. 'He always sleeps at home.'

'You've a key, haven't you?' he remarked pointedly.

'Yes, but I don't see why I should use it with you there,' retorted Jilly. 'It shouldn't be that difficult for you—after all, I'll be giving him lunch round here...'

'And where does he take his afternoon tea—Claridge's? Talk about over-feeding!' exclaimed Jean-Luc, throwing up his hands in disbelief.

'He's not over-fed...'

'Stop it, will you—both of you!' protested Linda, laughing. 'You're like a pair of squabbling children! I'm making coffee—and the first of you to make so much as a reference to that cat will be out on his or her ear. Is that understood?'

'Mais oui, madame,' murmured Jean-Luc, placing his hands together piously and bowing as he flashed Jilly a boyishly conspiratorial look. 'Now you.'

'Yes, ma'am,' she obliged, unable to suppress the mischievous answering grin that leapt to her lips. 'I'll change the subject altogether.' She glanced at her sister, now filling the percolator. 'How about discussing putting this layabout to work?'

She realised, too late, how appallingly familiar her words had sounded—the French could be rigidly formal at times and this particular one was, to say the least, unpredictable.

'Am I right in believing you have something specific in mind?' he murmured, his expression adroitly conveying she had indeed overstepped the mark and that only his magnanimity was allowing her to get away with it.

'Not me—Linda,' stated Jilly, her bravado wilting as she glanced nervously at her sister's back.

'I'm sure it wouldn't interest you,' said Linda with uncharacteristic diffidence.

'We'll never know if you don't tell me.' Jean-Luc caught Jilly's eye, raising questioning brows at her.

'I certainly couldn't explain,' she ducked out, rising to clear the table.

'Well, Linda?' he persisted.

'Oh, all right,' sighed Linda grudgingly, glaring at Jilly as she brushed past her. 'I'll show you something.' She flew out to the hall and returned with her briefcase. 'Do you know anything about advertising techniques?' she asked hesitantly, clutching the unopened briefcase to her.

He shook his head. 'Apart from having once read that sales can be vastly improved merely by changing packaging colours—nothing. I found that bit of information rather odd—naïvely assuming, as I had, that if a biscuit, for example, didn't sell, it would be the flavour they started worrying about, not its wrappings.'

'I think they should do away with all that ghastly wrapping altogether,' stated Jilly, placing cream and sugar on the table. 'Apart from needing phenomenal manual dexterity just to get at what's inside, it's so wasteful. And ecologically it's...'

'Jilly!' begged Linda in quiet desperation.

'Oops, I'm sorry,' gasped Jilly contritely, her hand flying to her mouth. 'The coffee's done—I'll get it.'

'I suppose it doesn't matter how good a product is, if you can't first of all persuade people to buy it—is that it?' asked the Frenchman, taking pity on Linda's obvious discomfort.

'Yes...I...that's not really an area I'm dealing with at the moment,' she stammered, sitting with the briefcase still clutched to her.

'Linda's company have just had the results of a very complicated survey,' explained Jilly, determined to make amends for her thoughtlessness. 'To find the ideal man to persuade people to buy—it's all terribly scientific.' She was amazed by the sound of her own knowledgeable assurance.

'To buy what?' asked Jean-Luc, sounding as puzzled as he looked.

'Anything,' muttered Linda, the single word devoid of any conviction.

'They've actually come up with a composite picture of this ideal,' launched in Jilly, determined to help. 'A man with allegedly universal appeal.' That had sounded faintly sceptical, she thought anxiously. And no wonder, she groaned inwardly, the whole idea was preposterous—a fact she had the uncomfortable feeling her sister might only now come to realise.

'I take it we're talking about sex-appeal,' stated Jean-Luc, chuckling softly. 'No, I take mine black,' he murmured, as Jilly offered him cream. 'Have they found the ideal woman to go with this man?'

'That's in the future,' stated Linda, sounding ill at ease. 'They have to find the man first, and see if the theories work in practice.'

Jilly handed her a coffee. 'Linda, why don't you just show him the photograph?' she suggested gently. She had never seen her normally self-assured sister so nervous before—which only went to show how important this whole thing was to her.

'OK,' sighed Linda, her hands shaking slightly as she opened the briefcase and removed the glossy picture.

Both girls were holding their breath as they watched the darkly gleaming head of Jean-Luc de Sauvignet lower in scrutiny. Then Jilly's anxious eyes flew to those of her sister as a small frown creased his brow before he looked up and silently placed the picture on the table.

There was an element of puzzlement in his gaze as he looked enquiringly at them.

'You seem to be waiting for some sort of comment,' he stated, the merest hint of impatience in his tone. 'I've told you—I know nothing about advertising.' He frowned as both maintained a stunned silence. 'I've no idea what I'm expected to say!' he exclaimed, picking up his cup and draining it.

'Didn't he...' Linda hesitated. 'Didn't he seem familiar in any way?'

'Familiar?' He gave a perfunctory glance at what might well have been his own image. 'Yes, I suppose he is.' There seemed to be relief in the smile he gave. 'Is that the secret of the appeal—that he manages to look familiar to most people?' He gave a soft chuckle. 'Does the advertising world hold that familiarity breeds persuasion rather than contempt?'

'He's not bluffing,' choked Jilly, giggling weakly. 'He genuinely hasn't seen it!'

'Seen what?' he demanded brusquely.

'That it's you!' she declared, picking up the photograph and waving it under the nose down which he was now positively scowling at her.

'Don't be ridiculous!' He drew back his head in order not to have to cross his eyes to glance once more at the picture. 'Would you mind removing that thing from under my nose?' he exclaimed, as Jilly shoved it nearer.

'You have to admit it's you—practically down to the last detail,' she insisted.

'You're wrong! I always wear shorts—can't stand that skimpy type of underwear he's barely wearing,' he declared, with the air of one proving a point beyond all doubt.

There was a split second of silence before Jilly let out a peal of laughter. Almost instantaneously, her light, silvery tone was joined by the rumbling bass of masculine laughter, every bit as spontaneous as her own.

Even Linda's lips began twitching as her eyes moved from one to the other of her convulsed companions.

'Apart from the underpants, Jean-Luc,' choked Jilly, pulling herself together with considerable effort, 'how do you fancy a stab at modelling?' Someone had to ask him, she reasoned, and Linda showed little sign of doing so.

His reply was a soft chuckle. And it expressed far more eloquently than words ever could that he took the question to be a manifestation of a decidedly offbeat sense of humour—one he could appreciate, despite its element of idiocy.

'I suppose your firm will now start interviewing men—till you find the right one,' he stated, his tone indicating polite interest as he helped himself to more coffee.

'Why should they?' asked Jilly, nodding as he stretched over to refill her cup. 'Now that we've found you.'

Linda, whose posture had been one of tense rigidity, gave a small groaning sigh as their guest's expression altered from amused disbelief to puzzlement and finally settled for one approaching outraged incredulity.

Anyone would think they had been guilty of *lèse-majesté*, thought Jilly impatiently. Who the hell did he think he was, anyway?

'Why so surprised?' Her truculent demand cut through the laden silence. 'Linda's only offering you a bit of gainful employment. After all, you're the one who admits to being a layabout.'

'Your idea of gainful employment and mine obviously differ,' he replied coldly. 'And, if you had actually listened to what I said, you would not have come out with your last, rather silly statement.'

'Please,' begged Linda, as Jilly took a deep breath in preparation for venting the anger boiling within her. 'I'd rather we dropped this subject—who'd like a liqueur?'

CHAPTER THREE

'I'M NOT being unreasonable,' stated Jilly, attempting to soften the indignation she felt from her tone. Linda's edginess for the past few days was beginning to concern her deeply. 'All I said was, if he's incapable of doing the little asked of him, you'd think he'd have the decency to let me know.'

'Jilly, for three mornings on the trot I've arrived at the office feeling like a limp rag!' exploded Linda. 'You *are* being unreasonable! Why can't you admit this has precious little to do with Charlie? All right—you lost your role in *Swan Lake* a few days after his arrival! Jilly, basic common sense has to tell you that was nothing more than coincidence!'

'Linda, of course I know that,' protested Jilly, even now having to suppress what reason told her was a completely unwarranted stab of doubt.

'If you know it, why do you treat the man as though he were guilty?' accused Linda. 'And don't start kidding me it's all to do with that damned cat!'

'But he does nothing for Charlie! He's never there! Linda, how can you . . .' Jilly broke off, her expression of indignation turning to one of complete horror as her sister slumped on to a chair and burst into tears. 'Linda . . . love, what's wrong?' she cried, rushing to put her arms around the weeping girl. 'Perhaps you're right,' she choked, racked by guilt. 'Perhaps I *have* been taking my disappointment out on Jean-Luc . . . blaming him even though I know it's nothing to do with him. Oh, Linda,

I can't bear to see my selfish stupidity affecting you like this!'

'Jean-Luc isn't entirely blameless—he's developed quite a knack of bringing out the worst in you,' sighed Linda. 'But it isn't really either of you—er—making me like this.' She gave a small hiccuping laugh as she searched in her bag for a handkerchief.

'But you're not yourself,' fretted Jilly. 'Why don't you have a day in bed? I'll ring the office...'

'You don't take to bed for what I've got,' giggled Linda, perking up miraculously. 'Or I'd be there for the next six and a half months.'

'At least let me make you some tea before...Linda!' shrieked Jilly. 'Are you saying...'

'That you're going to be an aunt? Yes.'

'I can't believe it...it's wonderful! Oh, God, I feel so dreadful about the way I've been carrying on over Jean-Luc!'

'No, it's mainly me,' protested Linda. 'I've been on tenterhooks; I've had a couple of false alarms before...'

'But aren't there tests you can have?' asked Jilly, puzzled.

Linda gave her a look that was positively sheepish. 'Until the other day, I couldn't bring myself to have one...in case it was negative.' She pulled a small face. 'But I've been feeling ghastly in the mornings...'

'Oh, Linda, why on earth didn't you tell me?' murmured Jilly.

'I wanted to, but I had to let David know first.'

Jilly nodded in agreement, grinning. 'So that's why you spent half the night on the phone to him...and all I did was moan about Jean-Luc not being there to give Charlie his supper,' she added with a groan of self-loathing. 'But I'll bet David was over the moon,' she whispered, giving her sister an ecstatic hug.

'Oh, he was,' chuckled Linda. 'He was all for getting on the next plane back, but I managed to dissuade him.' She got to her feet. 'Look, I ought to be going...and don't you think you should be next door, feeding Charlie? You know what he's like when his routine's disrupted.'

Jilly looked at her sister's smiling face, all traces of tears now vanished.

'Linda,' she began tentatively. 'I promise not to rant about Jean-Luc any...'

'No rash promises,' admonished Linda, giving her a gentle pat on the cheek. 'But you know, if you weren't so busy subconsciously blaming him for something of which he is entirely innocent and berating him for his neglect of Charlie, I'd think even you might begin to see that your brother-in-law, perfect though I consider him to be, isn't the only dishy man around blessed with personality. Jean-Luc has plenty in that department.'

'And much of it pretty vile!' Jilly clapped her hand over her mouth the instant the words were out. 'Linda, I didn't mean it!' she wailed contritely.

'The trouble is, you did,' chuckled her sister. 'But you're wrong, and it seems such a waste.'

'What do you mean?' puzzled Jilly, following her down the hall.

'You're stuck here, with practically nothing to do,' replied Linda, opening the front door. 'Yet when a perfectly stunning specimen of manhood happens to move in next door, all you do is fight with him....I call that waste.'

'But he's hardly ever there,' protested Jilly, laughing. 'Linda, I wonder what he does.'

'Why not try asking?' teased Linda. 'And don't forget, the fishmonger comes today,' she called out, as she went down the path. 'You'd better get another ton or two of fish for Gutso Miles . . .'

'Heck, I'd better feed him!' Jilly exclaimed. 'And tell him the fabulous news,' she called, with a mischievous grin, as Linda got into her car.

She gave the departing car a wave as she let herself into the house next door, one of six in the elegant Georgian terrace, then hesitated, frowning. She had expected her charge to hurl himself at her legs in his normal 'I'm half dead from hunger' routine.

'Charlie,' she called softly, popping her head round the kitchen door.

He had to be somewhere in the house, she reasoned anxiously, climbing the stairs to the first-floor living-room. Charlie was a creature of relentless habit and would never dream of venturing out without his breakfast in him. He was probably sulking somewhere. She pushed open the living-room door.

'Charlie . . .' The word choked to a small gasp.

Draped along the entire length of Lady Lou's fragilely elegant sofa, and spilling over it, lay Jean-Luc de Sauvignet—fast asleep. He was flat on his back, his long, dark-suited legs dangling over one armrest and his arms, stretched out above his head, over the other.

Lying across the sleeping man's chest, and now stirring lazily from slumber, was Charlie Miles.

Jilly stood immobile at the doorway as the cat glanced uninterestedly in her direction, stretched, and then began kneading his claws against the man's stomach to the accompaniment of loud purrs of contentment.

Still rooted to the spot, Jilly heard Jean-Luc de Sauvignet mutter softly in French as his body arched in sudden protest.

Ignoring both the words and the warning movement, Charlie kneaded ruthlessly on.

'Charlie, stop it,' hissed Jilly, just as a hand moved to swat at the cat.

Charlie glared balefully at the hand as it returned to swat him with increased force—then he bit it.

With a roar of surprise, the Frenchman sat up, toppling the startled cat from his body. His handsome face was dark with the stubble of beard and there were dark circles beneath the eyes that glared at his erstwhile sleeping companion, now arching his back threateningly.

Though she understood nothing of the rapid torrent of French being directed at the irate Charlie, Jilly was amazed to detect what bordered on grudging affection in the tone of those words.

'Did he bite you hard?' she asked, and immediately realised, from his startled expression, that Jean-Luc had been totally unaware of her presence.

Frowning, he inspected his hand. 'It's a relief to know this is a rabies-free country,' he muttered, his tone lacking conviction. 'What time is it?'

Jilly glanced at her watch. 'Eight-thirty.'

With a soft groan of disbelief, he dragged his fingers through the tousled disorder of his hair. 'I've had less than four hours' sleep.'

'That's hardly my fault,' observed Jilly unsympathetically. 'I assumed I'd be required to feed Charlie this morning—just as I had to last night,' she added pointedly. 'Look, if you're incapable of informing me when you won't be around to carry out the few duties required of you, couldn't you at least stick a note on the door to let me know you've crawled back at the crack of dawn? It would save me the hassle of coming round here unnecessarily.'

'Jilly, you realise your quarrel with me has little to do with my neglect of Charlie,' he stated, getting to his feet and stretching lazily. 'Your main problem is that you resent having confided in me and now you're determined to punish me for what you regard as a mistake.'

'And your main problem is a vivid imagination,' retorted Jilly, unsuccessfully trying to stifle the sharp guilt his words evoked in her... he had only hit on half of it! 'Do you make a habit of sleeping in your clothes?' she demanded, eyeing the wrinkles in the beautifully cut suit and launching into attack for fear of what guilt might cause her to blurt out.

'OK, we'll drop the subject, as long as you try not to nag, darling,' he drawled sarcastically, slouching past her. 'How about making yourself useful and rustling up breakfast—for the three of us, naturally—while I shower?'

Jilly was on the verge of telling him, quite explicitly, what he could do with his suggestion, when the memory of Linda's earlier distress nagged its way into her mind.

'What would you like for breakfast?' she asked quietly.

Jean-Luc de Sauvignet stopped dead in his tracks, then took three steps backwards to return to her side.

'Tell me, Jilly,' he murmured, his eyes gleaming their amusement as he looked down at her, 'did I dream it— or did you actually ask me what I wanted for breakfast?'

'Very funny,' she drawled, startled to find her mind zooming off at a wild tangent that suddenly understood completely why this man would have universal appeal. 'There's something I have to discuss with you...'

'If you think I'll agree to prancing around in my underpants before cameras, just because you deign to cook me breakfast, think again—I shan't.'

'It's nothing to do with that,' retorted Jilly, determined to keep her temper. 'As far as I know, nobody had any intention of asking you to do anything in your wretched underwear!'

'What, no underwear?' he drawled mockingly. 'What on earth would my grandmother say?'

'That's not...oh, go and have your shower!' exclaimed Jilly, pushing past him and racing down the stairs.

'You didn't wait to hear what I wanted for my breakfast,' his teasing voice called out after her.

'You'll damn well have what you're given!' she called back, a half-smile forming on her lips to mingle with exasperation. However reluctantly, she had to acknowledge a sense of humour in him—even if it were a particularly irritating brand.

She went to the fridge, the now piteously mewing Charlie glued to her legs as she took out his fish.

'I must say, I'm surprised to find you getting on with him so well,' she informed him, 'considering he's only fed you once since he's been here—and that was the wrong thing.'

Again she felt guilt swamping her. He *had* neglected Charlie, she reminded herself impatiently. And she hadn't *seriously* considered that he might be responsible for her losing the role.

Charlie butted his head impatiently against her legs.

'OK, it's coming!' she murmured. 'You know, for Linda's sake, I'm going to have to take a leaf out of your book...you're going to be an uncle, Charlie.'

She placed the dish on the floor and pulled a face as the cat hurled himself at the food as though ending a month-long fast.

'Yes, I thought you'd be overwhelmed by the news,' she chuckled, then immediately glanced nervously over her shoulder. She was at it again—talking to a cat!

It was embarrassing enough Linda constantly having to pull her up for it, but she found herself cringing at the thought of Jean-Luc de Sauvignet's likely reaction should he ever hear her.

Jilly glanced up from the cooker as Jean-Luc entered. He was now dressed in faded, almost white, denims and a navy sweatshirt. The stubble was gone from his face and an after-shower dampness seemed to accentuate the slight curl in his hair.

'I had to raid Linda's larder for this little lot,' she informed him, cracking a couple of eggs into a pan. 'Coffee was the only thing I could find here.'

'I must get around to doing some shopping,' he grinned, joining her. 'Do you mind if I help myself to coffee?'

Jilly shook her head, conscious of the warm, slightly spicy smell of him now filling her nostrils. 'How do you like your eggs?'

'I'm not fussy,' he murmured, peering over her shoulder to look into the pan. 'But I take it one of those is yours—one will do me fine.'

'They're both yours...'

'I don't like eating alone,' he informed her, his cool eyes challenging hers as he moved to pour himself coffee.

'You're not being asked to eat alone,' retorted Jilly, her tone sharp. It was bad enough having Linda constantly nagging her about eating, without him joining in, too—especially when she was making such an effort to be pleasant to him.

'What are you having?' he asked, eyeing her suspiciously as she added the eggs to the bacon and tomato already on a plate.

'Tomatoes on toast,' she replied, handing him the plate.

'I suppose that's something,' he muttered, carrying his plate to the table and sitting down as Jilly followed him with the toast.

She was uncomfortably conscious of his close scrutiny as she dished out her own meagre portion and rejoined him.

'You seem to have forgotten your toast,' he observed, his eyes openly challenging as he pointedly handed her the bread basket.

She took a slice of toast and broke it in half, her lips tightening as he then passed her the butter. She was trying her best to be pleasant—while he remained his usual provoking self!

'No, thank you.' She picked up her fork and began dissecting one of the four tomato halves that had now taken on the appearance of scraps on her plate.

'I wouldn't risk any exercise after breakfast, if I were you,' he remarked, each word dripping sarcasm as he liberally buttered a slice of toast. 'With that gargantuan feed in you, you'd find yourself plagued with cramp.'

Jilly flung down her fork and glared at him. 'I don't go around trying to sabotage your life as a layabout,' she exclaimed hotly. 'So kindly stop...'

'Correction: I gathered your intention was to get me gainfully employed,' he cut in.

'That was for Linda's sake... what I eat, or don't eat, is none of your business!'

'Let's just say you bring out...' He hesitated, chuckling as though savouring a particularly amusing private joke. 'You bring out my paternal instincts . . . so, why don't you be a good girl and eat up?'

As his chuckle deepened into full-throated laughter, Jilly threw him a look of pure loathing.

'I'm sure you're the only one capable of appreciating your excruciatingly feeble humour,' she informed him coldly. 'You're about as paternal as Charlie.'

At the sound of his name, the cat arrived to investigate, choosing Jean-Luc's feet by which to stretch out his huge body.

Fully aware that she was being unspeakably childish, Jilly found herself regarding Charlie's action as one of utter treachery.

With all her good intentions now abandoned, she ate the bland morsels on her plate in angry silence, every fibre of her envying the hearty breakfast being consumed across the table from her. To quell her hunger pangs, she began to fantasise. If he were to choke, it would almost make up for this ghastly start to her day. Provided, of course, that he choked to death.

'So, what was this discussion you wished to have with me?' he asked conversationally, having cleared his plate with Jilly's fantasies unfulfilled.

Buying time in which to think, she took a sip of coffee. Her earlier feelings of guilt might have been justified, directed towards anyone other than Jean-Luc de Sauvignet, she reasoned. On him they were completely wasted. But there was no way she intended crawling to him for the co-operation she now needed from him. If necessary she would abandon Charlie to his neglectful care, if it meant protecting Linda. Charlie Miles was more than capable of enforcing his rights.

'Linda's pregnant.' She winced at the unintended baldness of her statement.

'Which, I suppose, leads us back to my burgeoning paternal instincts...'

'Which brings us to the fact that our squabbling over your neglect of Charlie has been getting her down,' snapped Jilly.

'Oh, I see. This breakfast was your way of apologising for all your unpleasantness—whether over Charlie or whatever. Jilly, your apology is accepted...'

'I wasn't damn well apologising for anything!' she exploded. 'If anyone should be apologising, it's you! Surely you could manage to organise your hectic night-life to squeeze in a couple of feeds for Charlie.'

'And what if I can't?' he drawled.

'You could have the decency to let me know—I'd do it for you.'

'Jilly, there's no need to raise your voice. I have perfectly adequate hearing. Besides, you're disturbing Charlie,' he added piously, bending to stroke the cat who compounded his treachery by nuzzling against his neglector's hand.

To Jilly's utter amazement and mortification, she felt her eyes fill and her lips begin to tremble. She never cried—never—she told herself in panic. She reached out blindly for her cup and promptly knocked it over.

Only the fact that the tears had spilled from her eyes to her cheeks made it possible for her to see the pool of coffee spreading across the table top.

'Leave it,' ordered a quiet voice, as she lifted her napkin with the intention of mopping up the pool.

She froze, watching as he went to the sink and returned with a cloth to wipe the table, seeing his every action as though in slow motion.

'You obviously haven't a brother,' he murmured from beside her, then continued in the same, pleasantly conversational, tone. 'I have two sisters—one your age—both of whom swear there are times they hate me almost as much as they love me.'

Suddenly Jilly found herself on her feet and enfolded in a pair of strong arms. Given whose arms they were, she found them peculiarly comforting.

'Jilly, there's something about you that makes me tease you almost as wickedly as I would my sisters.' He cupped her face in his hands, his thumbs gently removing the tears still on her cheeks. 'But you mustn't take me seriously,' he whispered, the vivid blue of his eyes darkening suddenly as the ribbon tying back her hair loosened beneath the gentle movement of his hands.

Jilly took a small, sharp breath, holding it as he removed the ribbon altogether and began spreading his fingers through the thick golden cloud he had released.

She was still holding that same breath when she had the ridiculous thought that no sister would ever react in the manner she was now. Not with this sensation of panic mingling with an almost painful thudding of her heart—nor with this breathless excitement that had begun as a shiver and was now jolting through her.

She raised her hands, uncertain what it was she intended doing with them until she heard his sharp intake of breath and felt herself pulled roughly against him. Then her hands moved surely, guided by a will of their own, first coming to rest against the soft material at his chest, then moving to savour the firm outline of the body beneath them as his lips met then opened against hers.

The melting gentleness of that first instant of contact was lost in the explosive charge that surged between them, as though each nerve in her body had been ignited by a hot flame of expectancy. Jilly gave a softly groaned sigh as her hands slipped beneath his shirt to cling and explore against the tautly rippling muscles of his back.

Her mouth softened in acquiescence to the increasing pressure of his, just as her body moved in unconscious response to the hands that slid down its length, coaxing and moulding it to trembling awareness of the solid strength against which it was held.

Suddenly he lifted her high against him, till her arms could reach round his neck and her fingers tangle wantonly in the dark thickness of his hair. As he held her, his lips still locked in their passionate exploration of hers, her slim legs curled themselves like an imprisoning vine round his body.

Her eyes opened to gaze at the face now beneath hers, then closed again—a small shudder of excitement jarring through her at the sight of dark lashes, softly feathering in fans from eyes that hid their secrets from hers.

Her own eyes closed tighter, this time in protest, as she sensed the slight tensing of his body and felt the stilling of his hands against her.

'Jilly?' Her name was no more than a hoarsely groaned whisper. 'That bloody cat's using my leg as a scratching board. Charlie, get off!' he roared suddenly, his head momentarily resting against her breast as he glowered down at the cat.

Then Jilly was on her feet once more, her breath coming in ragged gasps as she dazedly watched him attempt to remove the implacably determined Charlie.

In the end it was she who knelt and removed the hissing bundle, receiving a vicious sideswipe from his unsheathed claws as she placed him on the floor.

She remained where she was, kneeling on the floor, her eyes blind to the angrily swelling scratch on her arm as the denim-clad legs moved away and out of her line of vision.

Charlie flopped on his side next to her, his huge topaz eyes totally devoid of remorse as he gazed up at her, then lazily embarked on his grooming.

She could hardly remain kneeling on the floor like this, she reasoned, panic jarring through the confusion of the excitement still rampaging through her.

Her hand rose to her lips in unconscious inspection of their tingling, almost bruised fullness. It was her own response that brought her panic...it was as though, hidden inside her throughout her life, had been a person she had never known...a woman whose body could respond in instant madness to the touch of a man as though that touch had melted away every restraint within her.

Nothing like this had ever happened to her with any of the very few other men in her life, she realised, but she found no comfort in the thought as the searing memory of lips searching lips, tongue probing tongue, burned through her and only increased her panic.

'I've made more coffee. Would you like some?' His tone stunned her with its casual ease.

'Yes...please.' The husky uncertainty in her own voice appalled her, since she had striven to match his matter-of-fact tone.

What other way would he sound? she asked herself angrily. It was probably the norm for him to have women going to pieces in his arms. Hating herself for the paralysing panic gripping her and freed only by the dregs of her pride, she leapt up, took their used cups to the sink and rinsed them out.

'Jilly, are you OK?' he asked quietly, his eyes not meeting hers as he removed the filter from the percolator.

'Of course I'm OK!' she snapped, mortified to hear her tone blatantly declaring the words a lie. 'No...I'm not,' she blurted out, unable to stop herself. 'I don't understand what happened just now...I don't behave like that...I've *never* behaved like that before!'

'Pretty devastating, wasn't it?' he murmured, removing a cup from her clenching fingers and placing it on the work surface. Then he took both her hands in his.

It was the sudden jolt of excitement his touch reawakened in her that made her leap from him as though scalded.

'Oh, no! I've no intention of going through that again,' she exclaimed indignantly. 'Anyway, what do you mean, devastating?' she demanded, her eyes wary and accusing as she watched him pour the coffee, his expression openly amused.

'What word would you have chosen, Jilly?' he asked, carrying both cups to the table and sitting down. 'Bring the coffee-pot over with you,' he added disconcertingly, interrupting her determined attempts to regulate her scrambled thoughts.

'Well?' he urged as, still concentrating, she joined him.

'I'm not very good with words,' she retorted, dispensing with her unproductive attempts and staring broodily into her cup. 'In fact, I'm practically illiterate.' She gave an inward groan as the words slipped out, wondering what had possessed her to utter them.

'Jilly, what on earth makes you say that?' he exclaimed.

'Because the law requires that they give you a rudimentary general education in specialist schools, such as the ballet school I attended,' she replied stiltedly. 'And rudimentary can be very rudimentary if you're as academically lazy as I was.'

'Jilly...'

'And another thing,' she babbled, determined to distract him from further mention of what had happened, no matter how big a fool she would make of herself in the process, 'I'm not normally given to bursting into tears! It's just that I'm overwhelmed by Linda's good news...she's been very on edge recently...'

'And I agree we can't have helped,' he cut in. 'We'll just have to do something about changing that.'

Jilly nodded, racking her brain for words to keep the conversation flowing along these safer lines.

'You can't have been feeling too great yourself, Jilly,' he continued, before her brain could oblige. 'With all this uncertainty hanging over you...Jilly, why can't you just accept the fact that I happen to know about your injury problems?' he asked quietly. 'I realise I'm the last person you wish to discuss it with, but you have to talk to someone...and I appear to be the only one who knows. I also happen to know you have an appointment at the hospital today,' he added gently—a gentleness that left her feeling oddly uncertain.

'Yes, I have,' she muttered, then groaned as she peered down at her watch. 'Oh, heck, I should have left by now!' She leapt to her feet in consternation.

'Relax, Jilly,' he murmured placatingly. 'I'll get you there—I picked up a hire-car yesterday.'

'Are you sure you wouldn't mind?' she asked hesitantly.

'Dreadfully—but we layabouts have to fill our day,' he grinned, getting to his feet. 'I'd better leave a note for the fishmonger, though—we can't have Charles starving,' he told her, chuckling softly.

'How on earth did you know...about him coming today?' gasped Jilly.

'My grandmother, despite your fears to the contrary, has me fully trained. Off you go and get ready.'

Jilly closed the door of the consulting-room behind her, then leaned wearily against the wall.

'Jilly, are you all right?'

She felt firm hands grasp her shoulders as her eyes flew open.

'Jean-Luc, what on earth are you doing here? I told you not to wait,' she protested.

'It's as well I did,' he answered grimly. 'You look ghastly. I take it the news isn't good.'

'Jean-Luc...please, I just don't want to discuss it right now,' Jilly pleaded, a brittle awareness in her of the arm draping lightly across her shoulders as she was guided through endless corridors and into fragile sunlight.

She looked up at the black clouds filling the horizon, sneaking up to swirl their dark threat around the struggling sun. Soon the sun would be gone, just as any hope she might have had was now fast disappearing. But at least the sun would recover to shine another day, she told herself comfortlessly as she turned to face the man beside her.

'Why did you wait?' she asked again, her words wooden. 'There was no need.'

'I don't know this part of London too well,' he told her quietly, his eyes sharp as they tried to penetrate the curtain of hers. 'I could have ended up driving round in circles for hours, panic-stricken at the thought of never finding my way home and consequently missing Charlie's supper.' A smile began dancing across his features as his eyes gave up their search. 'Besides, I was hoping we could have lunch together.'

'Don't tell me you can actually contemplate food after that colossal breakfast you had,' protested Jilly, wanting to hug him because he had produced a smile she had found impossible to resist at a moment when she needed every distraction to be had.

'We could share a lettuce leaf,' he suggested, his smile still working its magic as he led her towards the car.

'I hate to be awkward,' murmured Jilly, wondering if he would ever know the gratitude she was feeling, 'but today you won't get so much as half a lettuce leaf from me . . . I'm going to break all the rules and really eat.'

'Thank God for that,' he laughed, starting up the car and driving them, with the ease of one obviously knowing London like the back of his hand, to a select little restaurant in Belgravia.

'I suppose we'd have arrived here ages ago had you known London better,' teased Jilly, amazed to find how relaxed she felt as she smiled up into his laughing eyes after they got out of the car.

He bent his head to hers, his lips brushing against her hair before he led her inside. 'You know, Jilly, I like it when you break the rules—you should do it more often,' he whispered.

Jilly sat down, almost snatching the proffered menu from the waiter's hand in her haste to hide her suddenly flaming cheeks behind it.

She was now in need of distraction from the distraction he had so ably provided, she informed herself in muddled dejection. Trust her to make the mistake of picking on a man like Jean-Luc de Sauvignet . . . even if he was the only one available. His whispered words had been lightly flirtatious, and her reaction? She gave a silent groan—a raw sixteen-year-old couldn't have reacted with less aplomb.

'You choose,' she said abruptly, snapping shut the menu.

For a fleeting instant his eyes showed puzzlement, then he shrugged and beckoned a waiter.

'Melon, grilled sole and side salads for us both,' he stated briskly.

'Wouldn't you prefer something more substantial?' she asked hesitantly, guiltily aware how sudden her change of mood had been.

'What, after so colossal a breakfast?' he murmured, his eyes on the wine list.

He gave his order, then turned his full attention to her.

'So, Jilly, are we going to play childish games and pretend what's so obviously on your mind doesn't exist? Or are you going to behave intelligently for once and talk to me about it?'

Jilly began fiddling with the stem of a wineglass. She felt no anger at the harshness of his words—he had only spoken the truth. But he couldn't help her...no one could help her—the decisions to be made would have to be hers alone.

'I'm starting classes again—tomorrow,' she stated tonelessly, wishing she had been able to inject a little joy into the words with which she had avoided saying anything specific.

'That sounds like particularly good news,' he remarked, in a curiously quiet voice. 'Jilly, why is it I get the impression you don't see it quite like that?'

'I've no idea,' she retorted, then smiled at the waiter bearing their starters as though he were a long-lost friend. 'That looks very good!'

'You've no idea why you don't see it as good news, or you've no idea why I should get the impression you don't?' he asked, enunciating each word with sharp deliberation.

'Stop confusing me with words!' she snapped. 'How am I supposed to work out what you've just said?'

'Forgive me,' he retorted coldly. 'I keep forgetting—you're only semi-literate.'

'That's right! It doesn't take brains to dance—just good technique and an extra bit of flair!'

'Jilly! What did those doctors say to you?' he demanded impatiently.

'I told you—that I could begin training again...if I wanted.'

'If you wanted?' he exclaimed, slamming down his fork and flinging his napkin on the table. 'What the hell's that supposed to mean?'

'Jean-Luc, would you mind lowering your voice?' she hissed, glancing pointedly at several riveted spectators.

'Are you going to tell me what they said or not?'

'They said my body has unconsciously trained itself to protect what is a weakness in my hip...favouring the hip by subjecting my knee and ankle to strain...'

'And they're happy for you to go on subjecting your leg to such strain?' he exclaimed disgustedly.

'There are very few dancers whose bodies aren't subjected to strain of one form or another,' she snapped, her mind filling with the words of one of the specialists. He had stated categorically that her early problems with turn-out should have been indication enough to those concerned—that she should never have been encouraged towards a career in dancing—and had added that no art form was worth the pain she had obviously endured. 'Anyway, I can't see any point discussing this with you—

the specialists obviously know what they're talking about.' If only they had, she thought miserably. The one thing that had disturbed her most about their disclosures had been the decided lack of a consensus opinion—one observing that her body, having coped thus far on the whole, would probably continue to do so; another, in so many words, suggesting she cut her losses and abandon her career immediately; while the third had disconcerted her completely by making vague references to pain-thresholds.

'All right,' he sighed, nodding for the waiter to remove his barely touched plate. 'Let's drop the entire subject and start practising being civilised—for your sister's sake.'

'That sounds like a good idea,' muttered Jilly, startled to find her head suddenly filling with memories of those shattering moments of passion shared only hours before.

The session at the hospital had taken it out of her, she told herself, pressing her napkin against her lips and mentally recoiling from the lingering tenderness that began to throb in them. But, whatever her state of mind, it was about time she collected her straying wits, she reminded herself sharply.

'When did you . . .'

'I'd like to . . .'

Their words, spoken in unison, died into hesitant laughter.

'You first,' he murmured with a smile.

'I was wondering when you last visited your grandmother.'

'About four months ago—just before your sister and her husband moved in. I usually see her more regularly than that.' He tilted his head to one side. 'Why?'

'I just wondered...that's all.' It was the only question that had formed in the chaotic jumble of her mind. 'What were you about to say?'

'I was going to ask if I could sit in on one of your classes, if that's allowed. I'm curious to see you in action.'

Jilly glanced across at him, her expression registering total disbelief.

'As you pointed out—I can only accept that your doctors know what they're saying,' he murmured by way of explanation.

'I'll be very rusty,' she warned, capitulating and startled to find how much she wanted him to see her dance. To witness her doing the one thing she did with confidence, she thought with a stab of irony.

'But you wouldn't mind?'

'No—I wouldn't mind...you can always leave when you get bored.'

'Why "when", Jilly?' he asked softly. 'Why not "if"?'

CHAPTER FOUR

'I'M MOST impressed, but I'd no idea it would be that strenuous,' he had told her after her first afternoon back at class.

'Shows how much you know about ballet,' she had laughed. 'I'm so out of condition I could hear myself creaking.'

The second day, the class, which he again asked to attend, was to be taken by a visiting Russian, a renowned master from the Kirov.

'Today you'll really see dancing,' she told him, her eyes flickering around the almost full hall. 'Lots of the big names have turned up for this class.'

Including Carla Simpson and Justin Malenka, she noted, seconds before her erstwhile partner greeted her by sweeping her into his arms and dancing ecstatically round the practice hall with her.

'Who's the guy?' asked Justin, his eyes twinkling mischievously as he twirled her to a halt some distance away.

'My neighbour's grandson,' she laughed. 'He's come to watch. Justin, I do hope you're not going to make a jealous scene,' she joked, digging him affectionately in the ribs.

'Who, me?' he leered theatrically, then his face grew serious. 'Actually, I've been trying to get time to come round and have a natter...would you believe it, Jilly, I think I'm in love...I don't think it, I am!'

Jilly waited for his teasing explosion of laughter, but all she found was an expression of utter seriousness on his handsome face.

'Funnily enough, I believe you,' she murmured, a smile of delight on her face. 'Who is she, anyone I know?'

'She's nothing to do with this,' he stated, with a dismissive wave of his hand. 'We'll get together and I'll tell you all about her.'

He suddenly grabbed her arm. 'Oh, dear,' he chuckled. 'Carla's spotted your visitor.'

Jilly looked over to where Jean-Luc was sitting on a side bench reading a newspaper. A disbelieving grin broke over her face as she saw the breathtaking series of *fouettes* Carla was performing right under the Frenchman's oblivious nose.

'It'll serve her right if she breaks a leg, she hasn't warmed up,' observed Justin maliciously. 'Though I suppose I ought to stop her, I'm lumbered with her as a partner till you're sorted out.'

Justin's idea of stopping his new partner consisted of his sneaking up behind her and giving her a shove in the back that sent her sprawling gracelessly on her face.

'What the hell do you think you're doing?' snarled Carla, at last succeeding in distracting Jean-Luc from his paper.

'You should warm up before you start showing off,' murmured Justin solicitously, stretching out a hand to her. 'Or you could end up injured.'

'Injured?' shrieked Carla, furiously slapping aside his hand. 'You've probably broken my bloody leg, you great oaf!'

Jean-Luc's head ducked behind his paper once more, his shoulders heaving with silent laughter as his eyes rose over the top of the pages to twinkle into Jilly's.

'Carla, are you all right?' asked Jilly, anxious despite her amusement.

Carla glowered up at her from her ungainly position on the floor.

'No thanks to him,' she snapped, flashing a look of hatred in Justin's direction. 'Jilly, how on earth do you put up with him as a dancing partner?' she demanded. 'Let alone as a lover!'

It was the arrival of the visiting ballet master that brought Carla to her feet with an agility that gave immediate lie to her claims of injury. And it was his presence that brought instant order to the chaos of moments before in the large hall.

'I take it he's someone pretty special,' observed Jean-Luc, his eyes on the slight form surrounded by groups of dancers now that the class had finished.

'Very special,' agreed Jilly, sitting on the floor at his feet and removing her pointe shoes. 'I was lucky to have been allowed to attend the class.'

'Your foot's bleeding!' he exclaimed in horror, the loudness of his words drawing several amused glances.

'I'm out of condition,' muttered Jilly, conscious of the stares. It would be a waste of time even attempting to explain to him how common an occurrence badly blistered, if not bleeding, feet were among dancers. 'And that was also a class and a half,' she added, smiling up at him.

Her smile was lost on the man busily examining the shoes she had just removed.

'It's a wonder there's anything left of your feet— teetering around on blocks of wood!' he exclaimed in disgust.

Jilly grabbed back her shoes and stuffed them into her holdall.

'Jilly, I hope you're coming to my birthday bash—you did get an invitation, didn't you?'

Jilly looked up as she slipped on her shoes and saw Carla at her side.

'Yes, but ...'

'You must come, Jilly,' gushed Carla. 'And, of course, bring your friend,' she added archly, giving Jean-Luc her most winsome smile.

Realising an introduction was what Carla was angling for, Jilly obliged.

'You will come to my party, won't you?' purred Carla. 'It's at Francine's,' she added, mentioning a particularly trendy London nightclub. 'And it'll be great fun!'

'If Jilly can make it, I'd be happy to join her,' replied Jean-Luc, removing the hand still clutched in Carla's.

His manners were impeccable, observed Jilly, unable to suppress a small frisson of malicious glee, but his aloofness bordered on glacial.

'Well, are we going to her party?' he asked, as they left.

'If you'd like to,' replied Jilly half-heartedly.

'It's entirely up to you, but it might be a good idea, from your point of view.'

She looked up at him, obviously puzzled.

'I'm the one usually accused of never seeing further than the end of his nose,' he stated, letting her into the car. 'But you really take some beating in that department.'

'Do you intend expanding on that unenlightening remark?' she demanded, as he started up the car, having said no more.

'Despite the verbal abuse the gushing Carla dished out to him, I'd say she had quite obvious designs on your lover.'

'Justin isn't my lover!' exclaimed Jilly impatiently.

'OK—your boyfriend.'

'He's my partner—or at least he was till I was laid off. I suppose he was my boyfriend for a while, sort of.'

'Sort of?' he echoed, his tone weak with incredulity. 'Jilly, surely you know whether or not you're having a relationship—of whatever sort—with a man?'

'It's not that cut and dried,' retorted Jilly huffily.

'You're either attracted to him or you're not,' he pointed out mildly.

'All right, I'm not attracted to him!' she exclaimed.

If she were honest, Justin's kisses had always left her feeling curiously as though the pair of them had been trying to act a role—a feeling she suspected was mutual. And acting it badly, if her response to the man beside her were anything to go by, she realised with a small shiver of remembered excitement. She hurled the memory from her mind, searching for a distraction with which to replace it.

'Your grandmother has a theory,' she blurted out, silently blessing Lady Lou for the myriad of theories she tended to spout. 'About my problem with men...'

'You have a problem?'

'No!' she exclaimed impatiently. 'I...do you want to hear what she said or not?'

'I'm all ears,' he drawled, with total lack of conviction. 'Well?' he added, in the same tone, as she huddled angrily in her seat and gazed through the window.

'Why don't you just go back to France?' she demanded coldly. 'I'm perfectly capable of taking care of

Charlie and the house. And I'm sick and tired of your sarcastic witticisms at my expense.'

'Never mind, you'll be spared for the next couple of days—I've things to do. Happy?'

Jilly's eyes remained fixed mutinously on the window.

'Why don't you stop being so ultra-touchy and tell me my grandmother's pearls of wisdom?'

His soft chuckle broke through the silence that followed.

'Please, Jilly.'

She gave a small sigh of exasperation.

'No sarcastic comments,' she warned.

'None,' he promised.

'I was sent to ballet school, as a boarder, when I was ten.'

He flashed her a look that was purely sympathetic.

'Justin, and two of my other ex-boyfriends—for want of a better word—attended the same school. Your grandmother says research indicates romantic relationships don't flourish given that background...something to do with being part of what constitutes an extended family causing the subconscious worry that such relationships are incestuous.'

'My grandmother comes up with some pretty far-out theories,' he chuckled. 'Do you agree with that one?'

'I'm not sure. I've definitely never been in love with any of the men I went to school with, and I suppose our relationships, even attempted romantic ones, have tended to be somewhat fraternal.'

She shrugged.

'And you've never been romantically involved with a man outside that group?'

'No.'

'Jilly, apart from near starvation, bleeding feet and constant injuries—not to mention a probable subconscious belief that you're dabbling in the realms of incest—what exactly does dancing do for you?'

'And that's your idea of not resorting to sarcasm, is it?' she rounded on him, angry colour staining her cheeks.

'Why do you see sarcasm in my merely stating the obvious?' he drawled, the car tyres screeching in protest as he swerved into one of the parking bays near the terrace of houses.

'I suppose looking in on a couple of classes makes you a leading authority on ballet,' she hissed, leaping out of the car and slamming the door.

'If you didn't recognise the truth in my words,' he taunted over his shoulder as he strode ahead, 'you wouldn't be gibbering with rage—as you are now.'

'You're enough to make a saint gibber!' shrieked Jilly, running to catch up with his long, easy stride. 'Not everyone has the advantage of your pampered, over-privileged background! Most of us have to work, and work bloody hard...'

'Stop swearing!' he blazed, his face tight with anger as he swung round to confront her.

He had stopped so unexpectedly that Jilly went crashing into him.

'And I suggest you have your childish tantrum somewhere less public. Apart from several others, your sister happens to be doing a spot of gardening.'

Her eyes wide with alarm, Jilly leaned aside to peer round him.

Linda, her hands on her hips and an expression of tight-lipped disbelief on her face, was standing there watching them.

'Oh, heck!' whispered Jilly in desperation. 'Jean-Luc, how are we going to get out of this?'

'We?' he murmured infuriatingly, then grasped her by the shoulders as she showed every sign of launching into a physical attack.

'OK,' he chuckled. 'Let's kiss and make up.' He leaned down and gave her a teasing little peck on the forehead. 'Now, put your arm round me—we'll face the music together.'

The expression on Linda's face, as they approached, left no doubt she was not in the least fooled.

'I've a feeling you've disappointed the neighbours,' she announced, a wry smile creeping reluctantly to her lips. 'They were probably expecting to see bloodshed.'

'I have to shower,' said Jilly tonelessly, ducking from under the arm round her shoulder and racing into the house.

She hated him, she raged as she sped up the stairs. She hated every bone in his perfect, supercilious body!

The earlier, savage pain in her hip had settled into a bearable ache as Jilly let herself into the house.

The time had come when she would have to face the truth, she thought fretfully, making her way towards the kitchen doorway.

Her body tensed visibly the instant the husky deepness of a familiar masculine voice reached her ears, and tensed further as that sound was followed by her sister's soft laughter.

Here was another, far more urgent truth to be faced, she thought, fear stabbing through her as she leaned her head wearily against the door.

Surely even the easy-going David would be disturbed were he to witness what was developing between his wife and Jean-Luc, she thought miserably—because it certainly could not be put down to imagination on her part... yesterday she had overheard them planning to meet for lunch, and this morning his distinctive white sports car had been practically bumper to bumper with Linda's as she left for work. Now the pair of them were on the patio, whispering like a couple of lovebirds— words that would break off guiltily, as they had tended to recently, with her presence.

And it was none of her damned business, she informed herself, entering the kitchen and making an inordinate amount of noise as she did. Warning them of her arrival, she thought miserably as her mind was suddenly filled with the vivid, stomach-churning picture of herself once gazing down at the dark fan of lashes against his cheek.

'Tea, anyone?' she called out, noticing how quickly that raven black head seemed to draw back from the gleam of auburn at the sound of her voice.

'Lovely!' Linda's gaze remained fixed on the man seated close to her and Jilly wondered what message had been in her sister's green eyes as Jean-Luc replied with a small warning shake of his head.

The kettle she was filling overflowed as she tensed herself to face them.

'How did the work-out go?' called Linda.

No matter how she tried to conceal it, there was strain—guilt, even—in her sister's voice, thought Jilly, sickened by the desolation seeming to bombard her from every conceivable angle.

'Most instructive,' she replied, her words giving no hint of the taut bitterness on her face.

Today had been one of the most instructive—for want of a better word—days of her entire life, when the references to pain-thresholds made by the least committal of the consultants had no longer seemed vague utterances...his were the words that now made most sense to her. Where one had said her body was accustomed to pain and could tolerate it for the sake of her career—the other had rejected the idea of her even wishing to tolerate it. The third consultant had merely observed that should the level of pain increase, there could come a stage where her body would refuse to take any more...the stage that every agonised nerve in her body was telling her she had now reached.

'Jilly, you're limping!' exclaimed Linda, leaping up to relieve her of the tray as she joined them on the patio. 'Don't tell me your knee's given out again.'

'No, my knee's fine.'

'You're looking very pale, Jilly,' murmured Jean-Luc, his eyes filled with concern as he drew her up a chair. 'Are you going to be up to Carla's party tonight?' he asked, his smile gently teasing.

What sort of smile had he been bestowing on her sister only moments earlier? wondered Jilly with angry resentment.

'I'll be fine for this evening,' she replied, her eyes drifting towards Linda, seeking reaction and puzzled to find none. 'Have you heard from David recently?' she asked, her tone much sharper than she had intended.

'Yesterday—he sends you his love,' replied Linda, giving her a strange glance before continuing to pour the tea. 'Heaven only knows when he'll be back, poor love. He's got caught up in a round of self-perpetuating conferences.'

'It must be very frustrating for him—being stuck away from home yet dying to celebrate his wife's pregnancy with her. David will make a fabulous father,' Jilly added, addressing Jean-Luc. 'He's one of the nicest people I know.'

'I'm sure he is,' murmured Jean-Luc, patently perplexed by something in her tone. 'Jilly, are you sure you're OK?'

'Still feeling paternal, are we, Jean-Luc?' she asked coolly, shaken by the sudden wave of hatred washing over her. 'I don't think I'll bother with tea,' she blurted out, knocking heavily against the table in her haste to be on her feet. 'I could do with a long, hot soak in the bath.'

The startled silence that greeted her departure lasted till she reached the hall, then their soft exchange of words drifted unintelligibly to her ears as she flew up the stairs.

She had seen the interest in his eyes the moment he had seen her sister—just as she had seen similar interest in the eyes of other men. But she had never for one moment dreamed that Linda might respond—even to a man as attractive as Jean-Luc de Sauvignet.

Linda loved David . . . her marriage meant everything to her. But Linda had been meeting Jean-Luc during the day . . . and there was far more to him than looks . . . it might be the looks that attracted initially, but he generated a personal magnetism that would draw, no matter what his appearance.

Words and images were dancing in her mind as she lay in the bath, the warmth of the water doing nothing to rid her body of its debilitating tension.

Up until the past couple of days she would, had she been completely honest, have described his personality as exasperatingly appealing. But if he were using that appeal to trap Linda in his spell . . . he could only be described as evil.

Sickened by the battle raging in her mind, she remained in the bath till the water chilled her skin, then spent several listless hours dawdling over her dressing—knowing in her heart of hearts her time wasting was a means of avoiding facing her sister.

'Jilly! If you're not ready now, you never will be!' Linda called up the stairs. 'Jean-Luc's back and the taxi's waiting.'

'Why are we going by taxi?' demanded Jilly, descending the stairs with caution brought about by the unaccustomed high heels she wore. 'It'll cost a fortune.' Her words petered away as she caught sight of her dinner-jacketed escort at the foot of the stairs. All those hours of troubled brooding, she thought, as her stomach began churning sickeningly, and she had failed to see that her major problem regarding this man's relationship with Linda was one of blinding jealousy. Suddenly drained and uncertain, she grabbed hold of the banister to steady herself.

'Jilly, you look so beautiful,' whispered Linda, taking her by the arms and inspecting her.

'Quite stunningly beautiful,' stated Jean-Luc, sounding as though he might be having difficulty believing his own words.

'What did you expect—that I'd wear my jeans?' snapped Jilly, nervously smoothing her hands against the soft folds of the dress she had spent so long deciding on. 'Did you feed Charlie?'

'Oh, Jilly!' groaned Linda in laughing protest.

'Yes, I've fed Charlie—and no, I wasn't expecting jeans. But one thing's for sure, I'm stuck with you for the entire evening. Any man tempted by your unquestionable beauty will undoubtedly run a mile the instant you open your uncharitable little mouth. Come on, let's go.' He grabbed her by the arm, his eyes glittering their displeasure in an otherwise expressionless face. 'And we're taking a taxi because I don't drink and drive...I suppose you've lost count of the number of men you've driven to drink!'

'And I'm sure a wonderful time will be had by all,' groaned Linda, shaking her head in disbelief as she watched her indignant sister being manhandled through the door.

So much for his fears about being stuck with her all evening, thought Jilly angrily, her eyes filled with disdain as they regarded the raucous group some distance from her. He had discarded her almost the moment they had arrived...still battling verbally.

And now he was probably drunk—not that it was as obvious in him as it was in Justin, Pete and Sally...the whole lot of them, in fact, she observed with disgust. Including the entire band, whom Carla had insisted on plying with champagne, and God only knew what else, all evening.

Her critical eyes took in the room. What regular nightclubbers had not been lured into Carla's raucous celebrations had long since left—and who could blame them? she thought, her jaundiced gaze settling on their hostess, now teetering alarmingly on to the small sunken dance-floor.

'Oh, dear, Carla's not about to strip, is she?' murmured a weary voice at her side.

Jilly turned to find a girl she knew only as Pete's girl-friend taking the seat next to hers.

'I imagined Pete's dance colleagues to be somewhat more cultured than they've turned out to be,' sighed the girl, grinning wryly.

'You could hardly have expected this idiocy,' Jilly told her sympathetically. 'It's Justin's fault; his girlfriend couldn't come and he's drowning his sorrows, as far as I can see.'

'He and Pete have spent the entire evening arm-wrestling like a couple of kids, with that dishy tall guy encouraging them and keeping score—who is he?'

Jilly cast a baleful eye in Jean-Luc's direction and spat out his name.

'The name sounds French, yet he doesn't,' murmured the girl. 'I take it he's yours.'

'In a manner of speaking,' chuckled Jilly, amused by her new companion's drollery.

'Well, I don't know about you, but I suspect you're having as wretched a time as I am. I've come to a decision!' she announced firmly, grabbing a full bottle of champagne from a nearby bucket. 'If you can't beat 'em, join 'em. My name's Patty, by the way—I believe you're Jilly.'

'Patty, you're a genius,' laughed Jilly, grabbing two glasses. 'I toyed with the same idea, but didn't fancy drinking on my own.'

'I've never been drunk before, have you?' asked Patty, as she filled their glasses for the fifth time.

'No,' replied Jilly, after a period of deep contemplation. 'But I'm discovering it makes me aggressive— let's see about breaking up that ridiculous arm-wrestling party,' she announced, leaping to her feet and having difficulty focusing on her new-found friend from her sudden height.

'You're on!' giggled Patty. 'Lay on, MacJilly!'

Jilly managed to lead them into several tables on their short journey, but she continued undeterred.

'Peter,' she announced, grabbing the unfortunate dancer by the scruff of his neck as they reached their goal. 'Patty requires your attention!' She turned. 'And I want you, Jean-Luc!'

'Me, or my attention?' grinned the Frenchman, opening his arms in mocking welcome.

'Hey—Pete, Jean-Luc! We've not finished!' protested Justin groggily.

'Oh, yes, they have,' retorted Jilly, stepping lightly into Jean-Luc's arms and twining hers around his neck.

'What took you so long to come and rescue me?' he murmured, still grinning.

'I thought I'd leave you to play with the other children for a while. Now tell me, have I your full attention? You're about to receive your orders,' she informed him, gazing up at him and deciding she was in the arms of the most beautiful and exciting man on earth—even though parts of his character left a lot to be desired.

'You have every last particle of my attention,' he murmured, his hands playing lightly across her back and sending shivers through her. 'So, what are my orders?'

His words were teasingly lazy, as were the casually possessive movements of his hands, and Jilly wondered if it were not a trick of the dim light that made his eyes appear so shrewdly watchful.

'First of all, we're going to dance,' she informed him, pleased she had worn high heels because they brought her face conveniently level with the curve of his neck.

'Are you quite sure you're capable of dancing, Jilly?' he chuckled, grazing his chin gently against her cheek. 'Boozed up to the eyeballs as you appear to be?'

'I'll overlook that libellous statement because of your drunken condition,' she murmured indulgently.

'You mean slanderous—libel refers to written declarations...'

'I'm pleased to hear you admitting it—whichever it is.'

He caught her close to him, his throaty chuckle tingling against her ear. 'I was merely trying to improve on your literacy...do you think you could stop throttling me long enough for us to get to the dance-floor? Where we'll no doubt find out just how slanderous I've been.'

'I only nearly fell because I had my eyes closed,' Jilly informed him primly as they eventually made the floor.

'I believe you, Jilly, though thousands wouldn't,' he told her, drawing her into his arms, where she discovered his body was shaking with laughter.

'Stop,' she ordered. 'I'm not comfortable.'

He obeyed instantly, his eyes twinkling their amusement as she lifted her arms up round his neck, her hands cradling the back of his head.

'Comfortable now?' he murmured.

She nodded. 'Except I'll probably get a crick in my neck looking at you,' she complained. 'But you really are a most beautiful man, Dr de Sauvignet...though you're probably used to being told that.'

'Strange though you may find it,' he chuckled, 'it's not customary for people to tell a man he's beautiful.'

'Well, I just have—and you are,' she informed him sternly. 'And if you hadn't such a lousy character, you'd be perfect.'

'As perfect as you, Jilly?' he whispered, his arms tightening as their bodies swayed sensuously to the slow beat of the music. 'And stop pinching my lines.'

'I doubt if a computer would ever come up with me as an example of perfection,' she sighed contentedly. 'Or was it my lousy character you're accusing me of pinching your lines over?'

'The beauty, actually.'

'Good. Jean-Luc?'

'Jilly?'

'May I ask you a rather personal question?'

'Depends on what it is.'

'You know the other morning—when you said the way you felt was pretty devastating?'

'Mmm.'

'You wouldn't by any chance be feeling the teeniest bit devastated right now, would you?'

'I'd say it was something more than just the teeniest bit... Jilly, please stop interfering with the back of my neck, you're sending shivers down my spine... why did you ask?'

His arms had tightened almost suffocatingly and his lips had begun a slow, tantalising trail across her cheek.

'Because I'd have hated to be the only one of us feeling like this,' she managed candidly, the breath choking in her as she turned her head to capture his exploring lips.

Her head was forced to stillness by the hand that suddenly sank into her hair.

'Why not?' she breathed, feeling the corner of his mouth against hers and needing nothing but the heady excitement of their touch.

'Because,' he groaned softly, his breath mingling with hers. 'Because...'

Then his lips were on hers, hot and impatient as they probed her generous welcome in that brief instant before he jerked free, pressing her head suffocatingly into his shoulder.

'That's why,' he breathed heavily into her hair. 'And I think the time has come for us to leave.'

CHAPTER FIVE

IN THE taxi home she had at first tried pleading for release from the virtual wrestler's armlock in which he had trapped her body the instant it had snuggled against his.

Then she was driven to voluble abuse by his doggedly maintained silence.

Finally she resorted to appealing to his better nature—half-heartedly, because she was convinced it was something he was unlikely to possess.

'Jean-Luc, even if you let go, I shan't be able to move... I think you've paralysed my neck... you know how injury-prone I am.'

'Jilly, darling,' he began, as the taxi eventually drew up.

'Don't you "Jilly, darling" me, you great bully!' she fumed.

His answer was to place a brief, soft kiss on her lips before opening the door and bundling her out.

'And what was that supposed to be—the healing touch?' she demanded, swaying precariously against him as he paid the driver. 'Perhaps if you were to try it again, it might do the trick... beautiful Dr de Sauvignet,' she giggled, as he began marching her up the path.

'Jilly, we've got to do something about getting you sobered up,' he exclaimed impatiently, dragging her into the house and forcing her on to a chair. 'Now sit there and behave yourself, while I get some coffee on.'

'Jean-Luc, what are you a doctor of...or is it in?' she enquired serenely, her eyes following each movement of his tall, dark-suited body with undisguised pleasure.

'I could say it's in aiming for the knowledge of the eternal, but I'd probably send poor old Plato spinning in his grave with such a blatant misquote.'

'Why do you always play with words?' she sighed. 'Jean-Luc, you're not something ghastly...like an agent for the French MI6, are you?'

'I thought we'd decided I was a layabout,' he chuckled.

Jilly looked up, to find him at her side. To her surprise he was holding a most contented-looking Charlie in his arms.

'Charlie Miles, you're a very fickle cat...I thought I was the love of your life, next to your ma.'

As she clapped her hand over her mouth in a futile attempt to blot out the words she had just uttered, Charlie came to her rescue, leaping from Jean-Luc's arms and on to her lap, purring thunderously as he kissed noses with her before leaping off again.

'I think Charles has just made his preferences perfectly plain,' murmured Jean-Luc, obviously having considerable difficulty choking back his laughter.

'It's just something I say to him,' muttered Jilly.

'What is?' he asked softly, his hand cupping her chin and raising her eyes to his.

'Thank God you didn't hear,' she exclaimed. 'What's so funny?' she added uncertainly as he began drawing her to her feet.

'You are, Jilly,' he told her. 'Beautiful as sunshine and funny as a...'

'As a what?' she demanded as his words trailed to nothing and his hands began moving gently against her back.

'I think I've dried up, for once,' he murmured huskily.

'Trust you to dry up, for once, when you were in the middle of paying me a compliment,' she whispered, her voice as husky as his from the shivers his hands were sending down her spine. 'I hope it was a compliment,' she added, her arms creeping up round his neck.

'Jilly, I'll be forced to paralyse you again,' he warned, his arms tightening.

'But you started it this time,' she breathed, her fingers teasing the back of his neck.

'Yes...and I wasted my time putting on coffee,' he laughed softly, 'what you and I really need is a cold shower.'

'Feeling slightly devastated, are we, Jean-Luc?' she murmured, her mouth rising invitingly to his.

'Jilly, please...I was very wrong to start this.' he groaned softly. 'Go up to the living-room...I'll bring up the coffee.'

But his eyes were a languorous denial of his actions as he disengaged her arms and stepped away.

'Oh, all right,' she sighed discontentedly, and wondered what had been so hilarious about her words as his laughter followed her up the stairs.

Her eyes flinched from the sudden glare as she turned on the main light in the living-room, and it took several painstaking minutes of clumsy fiddling with the dimmer switch before the room was bathed in peaceful semi-darkness. If anything, it was now a little too dark, she realised, eyeing the dimmer once more, then frowning. Jean-Luc was right, she reasoned foggily. If it took her that long just to operate a simple switch, it would take a lot more than a cup of coffee to counteract...she gave a gasp of consternation. She, who rarely drank more

than a small glass of wine, had the best part of half a
bottle of champagne in her!

Tutting loudly to herself, she stepped out of her shoes,
made her way through the large first-floor bedroom and
into its adjoining shower room. She slid open the shower
door and stepped in, peering concentratedly at the lever
and its markings to ensure it was the same as that next
door. It was exactly the same—hot to the left and cold
to the right—she observed happily.

Jean-Luc had suggested a cold shower, and a cold
shower she undoubtedly needed, she told herself, yanking
the lever to the right and letting out a shriek of outrage
as water gushed down over her fully clad body.

As the sharp coldness cascaded over her, her shrieks
gradually turned to laughter and she threw her head back
in giddy delight.

'Jilly, are you all right?' yelled Jean-Luc, racing into
the bathroom. 'God Almighty!' he groaned, as he caught
sight of her, shrugging off his dinner-jacket and reaching
out for her.

'Come and have a cold shower, Jean-Luc, it's lovely!'
Jilly sang out to him, flinging her arms around him and
dragging him in with her.

'Jilly, stop it, will you? For God's sake, behave
yourself...oh, hell!' With a soft, groaning chuckle, he
pulled her against him, his lips hot against the cold
wetness of her face as they searched for hers.

'Oh, Jilly, you're a beautiful madness,' he sighed, his
hands impatient against her body, his lips bruising in
their hungry search of hers.

She was not aware of the exact point at which he
reached out and turned off the water. Her only true
awareness was of the almost angry insistence of his
mouth against hers, demanding more the more she gave,

and the sensuous message of desire his body was imparting to hers. There was a hungry excitement in the darkness of the eyes gazing down on her as he slowly drew off her sodden clothing.

'Why do you cover yourself, my beautiful Jilly?' he murmured unsteadily, as she immediately folded her arms across her naked breasts.

'Because I'm *not* beautiful,' she whispered, looking up into the face from which water still dripped as it plastered his hair to his head and gave him the appearance of a magnificent statue carved from marble.

The statue moved, dropping to its knees before her. 'Then I am the ugliest man alive,' he murmured huskily, his breath a hot caress on her stomach. 'You called me beautiful, yet you're blind to the beauty that is you.'

'Stop confusing me with words,' she whispered, her fingers sinking into the wetness of his hair. 'Jean-Luc, why do I feel like this?'

'Because you've had far too much to drink,' he murmured wryly, then tilted back his head and smiled up at her.

'That's not what I meant.' She began shivering as she spoke, and he immediately stood up.

'I think we should get you wrapped up,' he stated briskly, then gave a groan of disgust as he began removing his shoes. 'At least you had the sense to take off your shoes,' he remarked accusingly, then laughed softly as she immediately began apologising. 'Oh, Jilly, what am I going to do with you?' he sighed, taking a large towelling robe and bundling her into it before he began stripping off his sodden clothes.

Half watching his movements, half trapped in the memory of only moments before, Jilly found herself wondering at the ease with which he had slipped free of the passion which had undoubtedly possessed him so short a while ago.

She turned away and rested her head against the coolness of the tiled wall. He had called her beautiful, but his passion had cooled at the sight of her nakedness... and then he had covered her.

'Jilly? Are you OK?'

She turned slowly and faced him. The white towel now around his hips accentuated the deep golden tan of his body—a body without a spare ounce of flesh on it, she thought numbly, yet one that could never, by any stretch of the imagination, be described as thin.

'Yes, I'm OK,' she replied quietly. 'Jean-Luc... I'm sorry... I didn't mean to embarrass you.'

'What gives you the idea you've embarrassed me?' he murmured, his words sounding cagey to her suddenly alert ears. 'Soaked me—yes. But embarrassed me... Jilly, what exactly is going on in that beautiful little head of yours?' he asked in exasperation.

'Jean-Luc, there's no need to pretend you find me beautiful,' she told him gently. 'I know I got cross when you made remarks about how skinny I am... but I much preferred your honesty then.'

He flung up his arms in a gesture of disbelief.

'You and I seem to have a serious communication problem,' he exclaimed. 'Jilly, can't you understand that a man would only make the remarks I've just made to you if he meant them... unless he were incredibly insensitive...'

'Which you, of course, are not,' she observed, in a bitter little voice.

'No, I'm not,' he replied tersely. 'Looks are obviously a matter of taste... and to my taste, you would be perfect with a few more pounds on you. But that still doesn't alter the fact that you're a very beautiful woman...'

'You stopped wanting me the moment you took my clothes off,' she cut in stubbornly.

'Is that so? I suppose it could have had nothing to do with integrity?'

There was scorn in her eyes as she swept past him and into the bedroom.

He caught her half-way to the outer door, swinging her off her feet and throwing her down on the bed, pinning her furiously flailing body beneath his.

'Fine instincts are obviously wasted on you!' he muttered savagely, dragging his fingers through her hair and forcing her head to still. 'Jilly...oh, Jilly!' His lips began a frenzied onslaught on her face and body as his hands impatiently parted the robe that swaddled her.

Her breath became a choking gasp in her throat as her body flamed to life beneath his touch, every nerve within her aching in instant response to the swift violence of the passion possessing him.

'I don't want your integrity,' she protested wildly, her hands searching and exploring the taut contours of his back, holding him to her as his lips began nuzzling their fevered impatience against her breasts. 'Nor your finer instincts...Jean-Luc, all I want is you,' she choked softly, burying her face in the warm dampness of his hair, smelling the sweet smell of him and giving her body up to the sensations of tormented longing he was creating in it.

He began speaking in French, softly at first, as her lips and hands began their own trembling exploration, then louder as his unintelligible words of endearment became a hoarse litany of protest.

'No!' he cried out, anger in that single word of denial, as he roughly extricated himself from her softly entwining body, rolling away till he lay flat on his stomach a body's width from her.

Jilly lay where he had left her, the towel that had once girded him now a soft, discarded weight on her thighs. And she waited, praying for the words that would release her from the freezing paralysis now gripping her.

He wanted her; he found her beautiful, she kept telling herself as the sound of his ragged breathing filled her ears, drowning out the soft pant of her own breath.

And what man wouldn't feel desire, demanded a harsh inner voice, when gratification was so blatantly offered?

She drew the towel up over her body, burying her burning face in its dampness. What was happening to her? How could she possibly have behaved as she just had? She was conscious of holding her breath as she felt the sudden movement of his body. Then his hand touched her shoulder before rising to her face to drag away the towel to which she clung. The knuckles of his hand began stroking lightly against her cheek.

'I don't think you understand...'

'That a man can want a woman despite his finer instincts?' she asked hollowly. 'Yes, Jean-Luc, even I can understand that.' She gave a small laugh as she sat up, drawing the robe tightly around her. 'You know, that was my first experience of what alcohol can do.' The light-hearted giggle accompanying her words filled her with a morale-boosting relief. 'It will most certainly be my last. And now, I really ought to be getting home.'

'Give me a minute, Jilly, and I'll get dressed.' His words were muffled by the pillow in which his face was now buried.

'Don't be silly,' she laughed, a coldly observant part of her cynically applauding her acting ability. 'Charlie can see me out—you get some sleep.'

'Jilly, this is an area in the training of our young dancers that has always troubled me.' There had been genuine sorrow in the eyes of the ballet director as he had faced her across the expanse of paperwork littering his desk. 'I know it can be of scant consolation to you right now—with your exceptional talent, I find your case particularly tragic—but this is a problem that the ballet world now recognises and has begun tackling in many of its schools.'

'It seems such a waste,' Jilly had exclaimed, the terrible bitterness that had built up in her over several days now spilling over. 'All those years of training...and now nothing.'

'I know that's how it must seem to you now.' The director had risen as he spoke, and astounded her by going to her side and placing his arm around her in a gesture of sympathy neither she nor any other of his dancers would have believed possible from their granite-faced Svengali. 'But when the shock of this terrible blow has subsided—and believe me, it will—you'll begin to realise just how many openings are available to you because of those long years of training. And when that time comes, I'll be here to give you guidance towards the most fulfilling opening for you. Remember, Jilly, though it will be to your immediate family that you now turn for comfort, you also have a family here—and our love and support will always be here for you to draw on when you need it.'

And, for an instant, those gruffly sincere words had ignited the faint spark of a distant hope in her, remembered Jilly, taking her key from her pocket as she walked up the path and struggled to resurrect that earlier glimmer of hope in the abject desolation now swamping her.

'Hello, Charlie—feeling lonesome?' she murmured, as a furry bundle appeared from the bushes and began rubbing against her legs.

She picked up the cat, then let herself in, conscious of the terrible emptiness inside her. It was an emptiness that had been with her for days now, she realised, pausing to hoist Charlie more comfortably in her arms; never once leaving her as she had struggled to come to terms with reality...a numb deadness that little had penetrated.

'Except you, Charlie Miles,' she whispered, rubbing her cheek against the soft fur. 'Is that why you've been so loving of late—because you sense this terrible feeling of nothingness inside me?'

She paused again, this time by the open kitchen door, to manoeuvre her jacket from her shoulders without disturbing her purring burden.

'Jean-Luc, you're looking worried again.'

She felt the colour creep from her face as she heard Linda's softly concerned words, standing stock-still as part of her cried out to make her presence known while another part of her strained to hear Jean-Luc's reply.

It was days since she had seen him, and that last time he had been a shadowy, naked outline lying face-down on a bed...yet now, as that deep voice drifted to her ears, she felt a longing more savage than any pain she had ever experienced fill her emptiness.

'Perhaps—but it's a private worry...I promise you, it's nothing for you to feel any concern over.'

'In other words, I should mind my own business?'

As she listened to his softly laughing protests, Jilly could almost see the caress in his eyes as they lingered on her sister—the look she had witnessed that first time he had seen Linda, now bolder and more open.

'Come along, Charlie,' she called out, the unnecessary loudness of her words sending the startled cat leaping from her arms.

She entered the kitchen behind Charlie, her eyes wary as they alighted on the two figures—their chairs drawn so close that their shoulders and arms touched.

'Hello, Jilly,' greeted Jean-Luc, his eyes for an instant holding Linda's in a look that glittered with warning before he turned in smiling welcome.

'Hi, Jilly!' called out Linda, the guilty tension in her face a stark contrast to the forced lightness of her greeting.

'Hello,' said Jilly quietly.

Jean-Luc's eyes had conveyed their message and Linda had obeyed. Words seemed no longer necessary between them.

'Have you been to class?' asked Linda brightly, leaping up. 'I'll make some tea,' she added, without waiting for a reply.

'Come and sit down, Jilly.' Jean-Luc patted the chair Linda had just vacated. 'You look very tired.'

He might almost have succeeded in sounding concerned, thought Jilly grimly, taking a seat at the other end of the table, had it not been for the edge of discomfort in his tone.

'They work you very hard at those classes. Are you sure you're up to it yet?' he asked, his eyes narrowing in shrewd examination of her.

'I'm up to it,' she replied stiffly, bitterly regretting not having gone straight to her room. It had taken her days to face telling the ballet director... yet discussing it with Linda—Jean-Luc—seemed an insurmountable hurdle... especially now.

Linda turned and looked at her, her eyes troubled as a strained silence descended on the room.

'Jean-Luc brought round your clothes—Lady Louise's daily laundered them for you—they're in your room.'

'Thank you,' muttered Jilly, her eyes scrutinising the floor as though this were their first sight of it.

'I hope none of the neighbours saw you tiptoeing through the bushes in Jean-Luc's robe,' said Linda, her accompanying laugh strained.

'Why should you hope that?' demanded Jilly, her tone brittle.

'I was only teasing, love. They probably wouldn't give a damn if you decided to streak across the green in your birthday suit.'

'The point is, I didn't,' retorted Jilly. 'I merely had too much to drink and stupidly decided to have a shower with my clothes on! Why all the fuss?'

'Jilly, you're the one making the fuss,' pointed out Jean-Luc, his reasonable tone incensing her.

'Nobody asked for your opinion!' she hurled at him, leaping to her feet as he seemed to recoil in alarm from her outburst. 'Linda, I'm...I'm sorry,' she choked, racing from the room and up the stairs.

She had made a complete and utter spectacle of herself, she realised in horror, flinging herself down on her bed. And she might as well stop kidding herself the state she was in had everything to do with the disintegration of her career... much of it centred exclusively on Jean-Luc de Sauvignet. But she had allowed her anxiety over her future to cloud other issues—to preoccupy her to the extent that she had been unaware of the love sneaking into her heart for a tall, darkly beautiful stranger.

Even as the terrible admission slipped so casually into her mind, she was trying to deny it. Love was too important to happen like that—unnoticed—unwanted—with such devastating speed.

But it had happened . . . and, having happened, there could be no going back.

Yet it was as though Linda were on the verge of going back—on the love she had so joyously shared with David . . . her husband and the father of the child she now carried. Couldn't Linda see what was happening—or was another love creeping up on her unnoticed? Just as it was for Jean-Luc.

As Jilly's mind became filled with the handsome, laughing face of Jean-Luc de Sauvignet, there came too a terrible sadness for her beloved brother-in-law . . . what chance had David ever stood?

Her body tensed in protest at the sound of the light rap against her door. The last person she felt like facing was her sister—why couldn't she just leave her alone?

'Come in,' she called, burying her face in the pillow. She loved Linda, wanted to support her in what must be a period of agonising dilemma for her . . . yet there was nothing she could say that would not be tainted by the savage pain of her own, all-consuming jealousy.

'Jilly, I've brought you a cup of tea.'

Jilly struggled upright, her eyes wide with consternation as she watched Jean-Luc place a cup on her bedside-table, then sit on the edge of the bed.

'I don't want tea—what are you doing here?'

'You did say to come in. And I wanted to talk to you.'

'I thought you were Linda,' she muttered, drawing up her knees and hugging them tightly to her.

Beneath his tan was the pallor of exhaustion, she noted as her eyes rose to his face, then dropped immediately. Obviously this was one of those things that happened to women when they were in love, she mused listlessly— this noticing of each minute detail and fretting over any negative signs like a demented mother hen. God, she hoped not, she thought aghast—it just wasn't her!

Her eyes rose to his once more, this time glinting defiance. Of course he looked exhausted—worried. And he damn well should be worried, she told herself angrily—apart from being married, Linda also happened to be pregnant.

'Jilly, why have you been avoiding me?' he asked quietly.

'Have I been?' she snapped.

'You know you have. Is it because of what happened the other night?'

'Jean-Luc, nothing happened the other night! You gave that virtuoso display of fine instincts and integrity, in case you've forgotten,' she reminded him almost accusingly, while her heart silently asked its questions. Would he speak of integrity to Linda, or would it be love that took precedence where she was concerned?

'And you would rather I hadn't?' he demanded coldly.

'At the time, probably yes,' she retorted. 'It seemed like a good idea then; after all, I can't hang on to my virginity for ever, can I?'

'And I just happened to be available when the idea occurred to you to shed it, did I?' he demanded, lunging and gripping her tightly by the arms.

'Yes,' she replied, her eyes defiant as they challenged his. 'And I'd be grateful if you'd let go of me—you're hurting me.'

'You didn't complain of my hurting you the other night,' he rasped, suddenly lifting her forcefully against him. 'When I held you like this.' His arms tightened fiercely around her, crushing her against him as the harshness of his words reflected itself in the lips that took hers, bruising in their angry demand.

Though he gave her no choice, she knew her body would have followed his without thought as, with a groan of impatience, he heaved himself round and drew her against the length of him.

'Don't you ever think before you speak?' he groaned, as her mouth opened to his, her arms clinging as a breathless excitement seared through her. 'Have you really no idea what passion can entail?' he whispered hoarsely, his eyes glittering pools of darkness as his hands slid beneath her shirt to cup the taut fullness of her breasts. 'Jilly, it isn't a game,' he murmured huskily, his fingers never ceasing their delicate torment as he gazed down at her.

'Whatever it is, I don't want you to stop,' she choked, her body arching in wanton supplication as she felt a sudden stillness in him. 'You can't deny that you want me, Jean-Luc,' she whispered, exulting in the shiver rippling through him as her fingers played seductively on his back.

'I admit such a denial would be futile, given our proximity,' he rasped, flinging himself from her and leaping to his feet.

He stood with his back to her, gazing out of the window.

'I thought it was meant to be the women who played hard to get,' observed Jilly gloomily, trying desperately to adjust her mind and body to the sudden swing from heated excitement to emptiness.

'How many times do I have to tell you, sex isn't a game?' he exclaimed angrily. 'But you're right in that not many women offer themselves on a plate as you are doing. Hasn't it occurred to you that most men prefer to do the chasing?'

'I really wouldn't know,' retorted Jilly bitterly, hot waves of humiliation and disbelief washing over her. 'Maybe Frenchmen are more chauvinistic than their English counterparts,' she added, and immediately wondered what could have possessed her to utter so inane a remark.

'You don't seem to have had much success with them, either,' he drawled, dropping his head against the windowpane. 'Or did my appearance really happen to coincide with your sudden yen to shed your virginity?'

'I hate you!' she told him, her voice shaking with rage. 'I honestly hate you!'

'The feeling's mutual, I can assure you!' There was fury on his face as he rounded on her. 'You seem capable of infecting me with your ridiculous childishness...a man of my age doesn't normally resort to caveman tactics to prove a woman desires him...as I did just now!' He dragged his fingers angrily through his hair. 'Jilly, do we always have to fight like this?' he sighed. 'I don't think I've ever been in a dilemma more confusing than the one I now find myself in.'

And part of his dilemma was that he wanted her physically, despite the strength of his illicit feelings for Linda...feelings he seemed on the verge of disclosing to her! Panic surging through her, Jilly clamped her hands to her ears to blot out the words that would deprive her of her last remaining tatters of pride.

Her eyes were screwed tightly shut as the mattress jarred once more beneath his weight.

'Do you care so little for others that you're not even prepared to listen?' he raged, dragging her hands from her ears. 'Apart from anything else, what's happened to your resolution to protect Linda? Or aren't you worried how your selfishly petulant behaviour might be affecting her?'

'Let go of me!' she choked, tearing free her imprisoned hands and glaring at him in outrage. 'How dare you ask me that,' she raged, 'when I'm worried sick about her?'

'Jilly, what are you saying?' he demanded harshly, gripping her shoulders and shaking her.

And thank God he had shaken her, she thought in an orgy of panicked relief, as his action brought a semblance of reality to the chaos of protest in her mind . . . a chaos that had almost spilled into words!

'Jilly, what are you saying?' he repeated, with the desperate intensity that could only be found, if not in a man in love, in one very close to it. And his desperation had been brought about by her saying she was worried about her sister.

'Jean-Luc, I'll explain,' she sighed. 'But please . . . let go of me.'

She would have to tell him about her leaving dancing—the disintegration of her career now relegated to being no more than the lesser of two evils . . . the greater evil being one she could scarcely bring herself to contemplate.

There was a parched dryness in her mouth as she felt him release her. And her heart was an empty void.

CHAPTER SIX

'JILLY, why did you carry this terrible burden alone?' asked Jean-Luc, when she had finished speaking. 'You needed some sort of support—even if it was only mine. Why didn't you tell me?'

'Because I was frightened you'd tell Linda,' muttered Jilly uncomfortably, her eyes never leaving him as, with an exclamation of impatience, he leapt to his feet and returned to the window.

'Jilly—I just don't understand you,' he sighed, his shoulders tense and hunched as he stood with his back to her. 'How could you want this kept from Linda? How do you think she's going to feel when she hears?'

Jilly's lips tightened angrily—to him there were no feelings to be considered other than Linda's. Had he no idea what a giveaway his reactions were? Was he even actually aware, yet, that he was in love with Linda? she wondered suddenly, remembering how awareness of her own feelings had come as though from the blue.

'Jilly—answer me!'

'Unfortunately, things are never as cut and dried as you appear to think they are, Jean-Luc,' she replied tonelessly.

'Perhaps—but you'll have to tell her eventually. There are times when uncertainty causes far more harm than the actual knowing, surely you can see that?'

'Unlike you, I happen to look a bit further than the end of my nose,' snapped Jilly, bygone guilts parading accusingly in her mind.

'Do you? Because it doesn't show! To me you seem no more than a selfish little bitch who can see no further than her own problems—and to hell with the effect she's having on those who love her!' he accused, his face dark with anger as he swung round to face her.

'Don't expect me to be insulted,' croaked Jilly, her face deathly pale. 'Because you've just hit the nail on the head. The trouble is, you can't have any idea just how much suffering my selfishness has caused!'

'Dramatic though that statement is, it tells me nothing,' he rasped, striding towards her and towering, grim-faced, above where she sat huddled on the bed.

'Perhaps my mother did push me at first.' The words came out in a disjointed rush. 'But I *did* want to be a dancer... from when I was quite small. When I was offered a place at one of the best ballet schools in the country... I wanted that place!'

'And?' he urged grimly.

'Dad felt ten was far too young for me to go—it entailed boarding. He and my mother had terrible rows over it. She and I got our way... and my parents were divorced and Linda, at the age of fifteen, was deprived of the only home she had...'

'Jilly, for God's sake, what are you saying?' he interrupted harshly.

'I'm saying that my selfishness destroyed my parents' marriage! Destroyed my sister's teenage years... I was all right, I was away from all the trauma of it... I had what I wanted.'

'Jilly...'

'The other day, Linda told me she'd always agreed with Dad...'

'Because you were so young—not because she didn't think you had talent,' he protested, squatting beside the bed and gazing up in concern at her tense face.

'It doesn't matter why,' whispered Jilly hoarsely. 'She and Dad were right . . . it was all a waste . . . such a terrible waste . . .'

'For God's sake, Jilly! I can understand a ten-year-old perhaps thinking like that—but not a grown woman!' he exclaimed angrily. 'Marriages don't break up for reasons as relatively trivial as that!'

'My parents' did!' she insisted stubbornly.

'Why, because you were the most important consideration in their lives?' he demanded, sitting back on the floor, his face a picture of glowering incredulity. 'What makes you think you're the centre of the universe, Jilly?' he asked coldly. 'You weren't when you were ten, and you damn well aren't now! And the sooner you accept that unpalatable fact, and stop wallowing in your own inflated sense of self-importance, the better!' He leapt to his feet. 'I'm giving you ten minutes to get yourself together to come down and tell Linda—otherwise I'm telling her everything.'

'Just you dare!' she shrieked in outrage.

'Oh, I'll dare all right,' he informed her coldly from the doorway. 'I only hope you find the guts to make it unnecessary for me to do so.'

'Jilly, love, stop glaring at Jean-Luc like that. He was right to make you bring it all into the open,' soothed Linda, her arm round her tense-faced sister as they sat side by side on the sofa. 'But I'll never know where you got the idea that your going away to ballet school caused the break-up of Mum and Dad's marriage,' she sighed. 'Can you honestly not remember how things always were between them...the trial separation? I suppose you'd not remember that,' she mused sadly. 'You could only have been about six or seven at the time...'

'But all marriages have their ups and down,' muttered Jilly, part of her refusing to be convinced.

'Not ninety per cent downs, though,' retorted Linda.

'But you lost your home—you were shunted like a gypsy between them,' Jilly reminded her sharply.

'And I wallowed in it...for once in my life I was able to enjoy them—even if it was separately—without any of that ghastly tension that had become part of life with them together.'

Jilly's eyes raked her sister's face, certain they would find evidence of the falseness of those words, then filled with bewilderment as all they found was absolute confirmation of their truth.

'But the way Mum had to fight to get Dad to agree to my going away,' she protested, this time with far less conviction.

'Only because Dad was afraid you were being pushed—and, whether you like it or not, there was a time when she almost had to drag you to classes...and another thing—she wasn't above using you as a weapon against him...'

'You sound as though you hate her almost,' gasped Jilly.

'I love her,' sighed Linda. 'But I'm not blind to her faults. Jilly, even you must have noticed how your career took a back seat with her the moment she remarried.'

Jilly shrugged uncomfortably; it was one of the many things she had relegated to the furthest regions of her mind—never to be examined for fear of what examination might bring.

Then her eyes rose and met those of the man seated opposite them. His gaze was the watchful, waiting gaze of an adult and it had the disconcerting effect of making her feel gauche and unsophisticated—like a recalcitrant child.

'It wasn't because I felt I was the centre of the universe,' she blurted out, feeling compelled to justify herself to him, yet feeling even more of a child as she gave into that compulsion. 'I just felt I had to make something of myself as a dancer... to justify all the pain I'd caused...'

'The pain you'd imagined you'd caused,' he corrected quietly, before glancing down at his watch. 'I'm afraid I have to be going.' He stood up, his eyes on Linda who gazed up at him in consternation.

'But I thought now we'd...'

'No!' he cut in sharply. 'I might not be back tonight... I'll see you tomorrow as arranged.'

As Linda rose and walked with him to the door, Jilly felt an icy coldness shiver through her. There had been no attempt at secrecy; just that bald reference to previously arranged plans.

He turned by the door, his eyes meeting Jilly's. 'Would you mind dealing with Charlie?' he asked with a ghost of a smile. 'I'll try to remember to slip a note through the door if I get back before the morning.'

'No trouble,' muttered Jilly, her eyes turning from them as she heard Linda offer to see him out.

She wondered if she would have tackled her sister, had she remained. Probably not, she decided with an empty detachment, then leaned back and closed her eyes. But the darkness became filled with vivid images and detachment was no longer hers.

* * *

'I'm beginning to believe she doesn't exist! Far from telling me all—you haven't even told me her name!' Jilly, dressed in a white singlet and running shorts, was sitting astride Justin Malenka's powerful back in the garden. Her oiled fingers were kneading relentlessly at the muscles of his right thigh.

'I feel all sort of funny—talking about her—I'll not do her justice . . . for God's sake, Jilly, take it easy! I'm dancing tonight!' he yelled.

'I don't know why you didn't go to the physio, you ungrateful pig,' she chuckled. 'I've just about got you unknotted, but my fingers are about to drop off.'

'You're as good as any physio—besides, I wanted to make sure you were OK.'

'Three days on the trot, Justin—what do I have to do to convince you I'm all right?' she teased, reaching round and ruffling his blond hair. 'And still no word of this love of yours . . .'

'Jilly, I've been thinking—you should take up physiotherapy. Any dance company would snap you up with your background . . .'

'I'd need A-levels before I'd get on a course,' Jilly pointed out.

'And you'd be perfectly capable of getting them—I don't know where you get this idea you're dumb . . .'

'Justin, I haven't got around to thinking about my future yet.'

'It's about time you did. Jane's just taken two A-levels at nightschool . . .'

'So—her name's Jane!' teased Jilly. 'I'm surprised she puts up with all these visits I'm getting from you.'

'She's not like that,' he protested earnestly. 'And she's dying to meet you. I've explained to her that not all female dancers are bitches like Carla...oh, Jilly, I'm sorry!'

'Justin!' she wailed. 'If you're going to chew your tongue each time you forget I'm no longer a dancer, it'll soon be in shreds.'

'I must say, it's beginning to feel a bit tender,' he admitted sheepishly.

'So—tell me what Jane does for a living.'

'She's a secretary. Jilly, even with you I seem lost for words...I'd only known her a couple of days...and something inside me seemed to click into place.'

Jilly patted his leg to indicate she had finished, then sat on the grass beside him. There was an expression on his face she had never seen there before—and it was as though the handsome, slightly shallow boy she had known had now become a man before her eyes.

'Jilly, for the first time in my life I was frightened— no, I was terrified out of my wits—that she wouldn't feel the same.'

'But she does,' murmured Jilly gently.

He nodded, rolling over and sitting up, his face anxious.

'I'm working on boosting her self-confidence, though,' he told her seriously. 'She understands the hard slog that's a dancer's life, but she's also aware that I've begun to make a name for myself and I think it makes her feel unsure of herself...I suppose only time will prove how much more she means to me than any glamour associated with success.'

'Oh, Justin...I feel all weepy,' gulped Jilly. 'You know, Lady Lou is right—you and I are like members of a family—it's as though I'm seeing my spoiled brat of a brother become a caring man.' She flung her arms round him and hugged him tightly.

'And I'm not even offended,' he laughed, rocking her in a bear hug. 'I really was a brat!'

A movement by the french windows caught Jilly's eye. She looked up to see her sister watching them—Jean-Luc de Sauvignet standing next to her.

Justin's grip slackened as he felt her body tense in his arms.

'We have company,' she informed him. 'Justin, let's go up to my room.'

He gave her a puzzled frown before turning. 'Hi, Linda—Jean-Luc,' he called out, then leapt to his feet and pulled Jilly up with him.

'Hello,' called Jilly, gathering up the towel on which Justin had lain. 'Don't forget your tracksuit,' she reminded him, as he began dawdling towards the door, still clad only in his underpants.

'You two joining us for tea?' asked Linda, smiling.

Jilly shook her head, flashing Justin a look of warning as he opened his mouth to accept.

'Jilly...it's true confession time for Jean-Luc,' announced Linda, her smile faltering as she caught the fleeting consternation on her sister's face. 'Jilly...what's wrong?' she asked quietly.

'Nothing,' exclaimed Jilly. 'Look, Justin and I have to...'

'I ought to be getting along,' muttered Justin, stepping into his tracksuit bottoms. 'See you both another time.' He smiled at Linda and Jean-Luc as, slipping into the top and with a grim-faced Jilly by his side, he made his way through the kitchen.

'Are you going to tell me what all that was about?' he demanded, as they reached the front door.

'I don't know what you're talking about,' retorted Jilly, refusing to meet his eyes.

'You know perfectly well what I'm talking about,' he chuckled. 'Hell, I like Jean-Luc—but from the look he was giving me, I don't think the feeling's still mutual.'

'Love's playing havoc with your imagination,' retorted Jilly dismissively.

'My imagination doesn't come into it—he looked the way I'd look if I saw Jane apparently canoodling with another guy.'

'And to think I thought you'd grown up,' groaned Jilly, opening the door and giving him a forceful shove. 'And don't forget to give Jane my love—or perhaps it should be my sympathy,' she added with a grin.

But there was no smile on her face after she closed the door behind him, then slipped into the cloakroom to wash the oil from her hands.

Whatever displeasure Justin had read on Jean-Luc's face, he had misinterpreted its cause, she thought bitterly.

'Jilly?'

Startled, she glanced towards the open door.

'What?' she demanded shortly, vigorously drying her hands.

'I just came to make sure you weren't about to slope off to your room,' stated Jean-Luc quietly.

'If I feel like going to my room, that's precisely where I'll go,' she snapped, swinging round to face him. Then she gave an involuntary gasp, realising how studiously she had avoided actually looking into his face until this moment. 'Jean-Luc, you look ghastly! What's wrong?' she blurted out, regretting the words the instant they were uttered.

'Nothing's wrong,' he muttered, as though uttering a magic formula that banished the existence of the dark rings beneath his eyes and the sudden gauntness that seemed to have sharpened his features in the three days since she had last seen him. 'Linda's made tea—there's something she can't wait to show you—God knows why.'

'To show me?' echoed Jilly weakly, her steps blindly following his while her mind instructed her to flee.

'Jilly! Just wait till you see what I have here!' chuckled Linda, gleefully waving a newspaper. 'And he's just as photogenic as I thought he'd be!'

Jilly looked in stunned bewilderment from her sister to the Frenchman, whose face was a picture of disgruntled embarrassment.

And no wonder he looked embarrassed, thought Jilly numbly, if what she suspected she was about to hear was true.

'I told you all you'd have to do was bat your eyes at him to get him to do it,' she muttered, the stiffness in her lips robbing her words of the jocularity she had tried to inject into them.

'Jilly, what on earth...' began Linda, only to be abruptly cut short by Jean-Luc.

'For God's sake, Linda, I didn't think you could be this childish,' he snapped, flinging himself down on a chair while Jilly gazed speechlessly at the newspaper her grinning sister shoved into her hands.

He was photogenic all right, she thought dazedly, her eyes dropping from the familiar laughing features to the print below.

'Dr Jean-Luc de Sauvignet, a young man with the nobility of two great nations coursing through his veins,' began the blurb, then went on to reel off his pedigree... almost as though they were describing the championship breed of dog at Crufts, thought Jilly in disbelief—Lady Lou would probably have a fit, if ever she read this. She frowned as she read on.

'One of France's most gifted mathematicians, Dr de Sauvignet was yesterday named as the winner of the prestigious Chauvenet Prize awarded by the Mathematical Association of America...'

'Talk about hiding his light under a bushel!' chortled Linda. 'And to think he almost had us convinced he was a layabout!'

'For heaven's sake, Linda,' groaned Jean-Luc, patently not in the least amused.

'Why wouldn't you tell us you were a mathematician?' asked Jilly quietly, placing the newspaper on the table.

'You thought you were going to read that I'd bamboozled him into signing up for a modelling career—go on, admit you did, Jilly!' giggled Linda.

'Even Jilly couldn't possibly have thought that,' exclaimed Jean-Luc dismissively, hesitating as he caught sight of the expression on Jilly's face. 'My God...you didn't actually think that?' he gasped in horror.

'What do you mean, "even Jilly"?' she demanded angrily. 'And what's so terribly special about you that I shouldn't think that? Just who the hell do you think you are anyway, Jean-Luc?'

'Jilly!' gasped Linda, her face a picture of shocked disbelief as she sank weakly on to a chair. 'What on earth's got into you? This was just intended as a harmless bit of fun...I was only teasing Jean-Luc...'

'Leave her, Linda. Let her have her tantrum,' advised Jean-Luc coldly, getting to his feet. 'Jilly, you ask why I avoided telling you what I do—I did so because it's struggle enough trying to get an intelligent adult to understand precisely what it is a mathematician does...to attempt explaining to a petulant child would have been a waste of breath.' With a parting look of pure disgust, he turned and strode to the door. 'I'm sorry, Linda, but I haven't your patience. I'll see myself out.'

'And my patience just happens to have run out,' said Linda in a shaking voice, as the front door slammed behind him. 'For years now, it's been a dream of mine to get to know my only sister once more. The only trouble is—I've become an adult in those intervening years...whereas you've remained a child.' Her voice almost broke. 'Not the sweet-natured child I once knew—but a self-centred, bad-tempered, petulant child. Yes, I know you've had a terrible deal, but you wouldn't let Jean-Luc or me anywhere near you to cushion it, you went out of your way to be as unpleasant as you possibly could to the two people who most wanted to help you.'

'Two people?' demanded Jilly. 'Linda, I didn't mean to hurt you. But as for Jean-Luc, what with his hectic nightlife and his being at your beck and call during the day, he's never been around to offer any help...even if I'd wanted it.'

'Yes—two people!' exclaimed Linda angrily. 'And as for his being at my beck and call—it was all for you! The man became so concerned for your well-being that he felt obliged to confide in me. And before you start castigating him for breaking his word to you—he did so only after a great deal of soul-searching. All he's had in return for his pains is unmitigated bitchiness from you! No! I haven't finished!' she exploded, as Jilly attempted to speak. 'Far from being at my beck and call, Jean-Luc's been dragging me all over London, whenever I have time—looking for alternative specialists for you, though expert opinion is that you're already seeing the best in that field.'

'It's not me he's so worried about...can't you see?'

'No, I damn well can't!' exclaimed Linda bitterly.

'Jean-Luc's only worried about me in relation to how my problems affect you. Linda, he's half-way to being in love with you—if not already there.'

'My God—I don't believe I'm hearing this,' groaned Linda. 'Jilly, don't you think it's about time you opened your eyes—grew up?' she exclaimed wearily. 'If Jean-Luc was half-way to being in love with anyone, it was you...at the beginning. Why else do you think he put up with your atrocious behaviour? God knows, though, you've done everything a woman possibly could to cure him,' she added bitterly, though the anger was dying in her eyes even as they met Jilly's. 'I love you too much, Jilly, to stand by and watch you become embittered and selfish...I know the person I've been seeing lately just isn't the real you.'

'Linda, I've never been so mixed up...so frightened in my life before. It's not because of what's happened to my career...I could have handled that fifty times over rather than this.'

'Rather than what, love?' demanded Linda anxiously.

'Than...God, I feel terrible just admitting it. Linda, I knew you and Jean-Luc were meeting...I kept thinking of poor David...'

'Poor David? For heaven's sake, Jilly, you didn't think Jean-Luc and I were...oh, Jilly, you crazy little idiot!' she groaned. 'It's a wonder I haven't my hands round your throat for even thinking such a thing. Oh, Jilly!'

As she watched disbelief, consternation, then a rueful smile chase their way across her sister's face, Jilly was filled with a sickening guilt. She must have been out of her mind to have had even a single doubt...Linda was so in love with David she was completely oblivious to the signs of Jean-Luc's feelings towards her.

'Linda...can you ever forgive me?' she croaked. 'I don't know how I allowed my imagination to run amok like that.'

'And because it did, I suppose I can almost understand your ghastly behaviour,' sighed Linda, then frowned. 'Though I doubt if Jean-Luc's going to feel too charitable...'

'Linda—you wouldn't tell him!' gasped Jilly.

'It would damn well serve you right if I did,' Linda chuckled. Then the frown returned to her brow, deepening. 'Jilly, I'm worried about Jean-Luc—there's something quite definitely wrong with him,' she stated suddenly. 'I can't put my finger on it exactly, but for the past couple of days he's been...I don't know...noticeably jittery and distracted. It's almost as though he was glad to have something to throw himself into—tracking down new specialists for you. Jilly, he's genuinely worried about you, but he was using that worry like a desperately needed distraction from something else...he's looking almost haggard.'

'Yes, I'd noticed that,' said Jilly quietly, shaken by the all-pervading fear her sister's words had instilled in her. 'Not having seen him for a few days...it hit me immediately.' It wasn't that there was anything physically wrong with him, she tried comforting herself...Jean-Luc was a man of integrity; one who would be profoundly disturbed to find himself in love with a woman he had no right to love...her clumsy attempt at rationalisation, she found, brought scant comfort.

'Why don't you try making it up with him?' suggested Linda gently. 'You could say you've been in a lot of pain...no, we don't want to tempt fate...I know, say you've been taking medicine that didn't agree with you . . .'

'Linda!' groaned Jilly, smiling despite herself. 'You're even worse at lying than I am.' She broke off as she saw the deep anxiety on her sister's face. 'But you're really worried about him, I can see,' she whispered, alarm welling in her once more.

'Jilly, there's definitely something troubling him. And it damn well isn't that he thinks he's in love with me, either,' finished Linda sharply.

'I was wondering if you'd like to come round for supper,' stated Jilly, conscious of how unnatural and strained her voice sounded as she stood on Lady Lou's doorstep and tried desperately to close her mind to the total rejection on the face of the man holding open the door. 'I'm afraid it's only me—Linda's having a soak and an early night.' Words guaranteed to make him turn down the invitation, she pointed out bitterly to herself.

'I'm expecting a phone call,' he stated, his eyes chillingly remote as they gazed down on her.

'It was just an idea,' shrugged Jilly. 'A sort of prelude to my apology . . .' Her words petered away, but at least she had let him know she was prepared to apologise.

'I was about to have an omelette—you're welcome to join me.'

'Are you sure? I mean, I wouldn't . . .'

'Jilly, don't tell me you're backing down on that offer of an apology already,' he murmured wryly, opening the door wide for her to enter.

As she stepped in, she found herself trying to conjure up those days when her heart had always lightened on entering this familiar place of friendship . . . it seemed so long ago.

'You've no idea how much I miss your grandmother.' The words seemed to slip out of their own accord as she followed his tall figure into the large open-plan kitchen.

'Still feeling the need to confide in her?' enquired Jean-Luc, as he attempted stacking the sheaf of papers strewn over the table—on some of which Charlie was contentedly sprawled.

'No—I didn't mean it like that,' protested Jilly belatedly, watching in fascination. 'You know, she may spoil Charlie, but she doesn't allow him on the table,' she pointed out as the cat thudded a proprietorial paw down on the papers beside him.

'He takes no notice of me when I tell him to get off... Charlie, cut it out!' growled Jean-Luc, as the cat pounced on the papers he was trying to extricate.

'He thinks you're playing,' chuckled Jilly, as man and cat glared warningly at one another.

'Perhaps you'd like to convince him otherwise,' retorted Jean-Luc, relinquishing his hold on the trapped papers and passing those he held to Jilly. 'I'll see to the food.'

Jilly stared down at the papers in her hand. His writing was surprisingly neat and legible—or rather it would have been legible had she understood French and had any idea of the meaning of the strange hieroglyphics interspersing the prose.

'You're right,' she muttered, almost to herself. 'Even if I understood the French, the maths would be double Dutch to me.'

'I thought all ballet dancers spoke French,' he stated, as Charlie simplified her task by leaping off the table.

'Ballet terms are all in French—though I doubt if I'd get very far in France by reciting them. Do you teach maths?'

'I do some work with postgraduate students whose studies lie within my field. Jilly, my remarks about your not being capable of understanding what I do were unkind and uncalled-for.'

'Hardly uncalled-for, when they were true,' she contradicted as she began laying the table.

'If it's any consolation—pure mathematics is so minutely specialised that few mathematicians have any comprehension of one another's fields.'

Jilly said nothing—at least he was attempting to be kind over her ignorance.

'I'm not just saying that, either,' he continued, as if reading her mind. 'There are so many different fields in mathematics—though some of them overlap slightly... and when they do it's like...' he paused, plainly searching for words '...it's like a Russian and an Italian meeting— neither speaking the other's language, but able to communicate only because each happens to have a smattering of English... would you mind opening that wine? The food will be ready any moment now.'

They were half-way through their excellent meal—their conversation noticeably stilted—when the phone rang.

'Yes, speaking,' he barked as he quickly leaned over and snatched up the receiver before it had even rung a second time.

As Jilly watched him, she had the oddest sensation of actually witnessing the tension seep into every muscle of his body—till the erratic beating of the small pulse at the curve of his neck was the only movement visible in him.

'I was under the impression we'd know today... yes, yes—I can understand that...'

The hand that eventually replaced the receiver was shaking badly, and Jilly immediately found herself dragging her eyes from it—not knowing whether she should remark on the obvious state he was in, or go through the pretence of appearing not to have noticed.

But the effect of the phone call on him was so severe that she would have had to be blind not to see it—not to be aware of the disturbingly compulsive action of those long, slim fingers as they nervously shredded the bread on his side-plate.

'Jean-Luc, I know I've always reacted most ungraciously whenever you've offered me an ear...but you need one now...and I'm here.' Her eyes met his, widening in alarm as they caught the bleakness of a terrible fear in his.

She saw her alarm register with him, and saw too the monumental exertion it took for him to get a grip on himself, and she saw the moment when he succeeded and the fear began receding from his eyes.

'Perhaps it's not so much an ear that I need, Jilly, as distraction,' he muttered hollowly.

'Why don't you take the rest of the wine up to the living-room?' suggested Jilly, trying to mask her anxiety with brightness and not succeeding too well. 'I'll clear this and get the coffee on.'

He nodded, his expression now disturbingly blank.

'And that was a delicious omelette, Jean-Luc—the best I've ever tasted.'

'I'm glad,' he muttered vaguely, rising and looking round him. 'Charlie!'

Jilly was no longer bothering to try concealing her anxiety as she watched him looking around, repeatedly calling for the cat.

'There you are!' he exclaimed, as Charlie strolled lazily from beneath the table and sat gazing up at him.

When Jean-Luc stooped and picked him up, Charlie made no objection and his large topaz eyes gazed enigmatically over the man's shoulder at Jilly as he was carried from the room, his tabby stripes blending into the darkness of the head that seemed to nestle as though for comfort against him.

And he hadn't taken the wine with him, thought Jilly distractedly as she quickly began clearing the table. Linda was right—there was something wrong with him... something terribly wrong.

She had gone as close as she possibly could to actually asking him what it was, she fretted, as she waited for the coffee to percolate. He seemed to have no intention of confiding in her—it was almost as though it were to Charlie he were turning for comfort.

Several times, as she prepared the tray, she had to stop—clenching and unclenching her hands in an attempt to ease their violent shaking.

To think that she had once fantasised about falling in love...imagining the ecstatic joy that would become hers through loving. Her fantasies would have seemed more like nightmares had she had any inkling of what the reality was to be. Trust her to fall in love with a man whose practical replica a computer had come up with as an example of what almost amounted to male perfection; a man who was an intellectual giant to boot; and a man who, despite Linda's protestations to the contrary, she still suspected was half—if not completely— in love with her sister.

'Lady Lou, how could you have done this to me?' she whispered plaintively as she added the wine and glasses to the tray. 'He's your favourite—you might have known I'd be dumb enough to lose my heart to him!'

Jean-Luc was sprawled along the sofa—the sofa that was a good foot shorter than his lithe body—and Charlie Miles was curled up on his chest, just as he had been one morning that now seemed a lifetime ago.

'I brought up the rest of the wine,' she said softly, placing the tray on the onyx-topped coffee-table.

'Thanks,' he acknowledged, not stirring.

'Jean-Luc?'

'Jilly.'

'When's your grandmother coming back?'

'Why?' He sat up, swinging his legs off the arm-rest and shifting an uncharacteristically docile Charlie into his arms. 'Why do you keep on about her return?'

'No real reason,' she replied soothingly, disturbed to find that the tension in him had, if anything, increased. 'I just miss her a lot. Do you want your coffee black?'

He nodded. 'Jilly, do I make you nervous?' he demanded suddenly.

'No—why?' She could have kicked herself for adding that 'why', given the underlying aggression in his question.

'Because you're acting as though I do. It's as though this business over your career has stripped the self-confidence from you, and God knows, you had little enough of that to start with, as far as I can see.'

'Considering you scarcely know me, you're hardly qualified to judge,' snapped Jilly, slopping his coffee in its saucer as she angrily shoved it towards him.

There was no way she could possibly handle him in this mood, she told herself. She loved him all right, but she had no intention of being his whipping boy, no matter what might be troubling him.

'Am I not?' he snapped back at her. 'Self-confident women don't describe themselves as practically illiterate; neither are they ashamed of their bodies without good reason, and they certainly don't try offloading their virginity on the first man who happens to turn them on sexually.'

As she struggled for composure, it was that Charlie seemed to be glaring at her with as much malevolence as the man in whose arms he was so treacherously settled that finally defeated her.

'For your information, I intend furthering my career. Justin and I were discussing...'

'I wondered when we'd get round to young Nureyev,' he leapt in. 'Tell me, does he always prance around the garden in his jock-strap?'

'He was in his shorts!' retorted Jilly furiously. 'And if he'd been naked it would have been none of your business. It's funny how that article—so full of the size of your intellect—made no mention of the colossal magnitude of your male ego!' she raged. 'It took alcohol to get me to find you physically attractive—a stimulus I don't need with Justin!'

'Been indulging in a spot of incest, have you, Jilly?' he drawled, his eyes glittering.

'Fortunately that theory fell to pieces the moment...the moment we made love,' spat Jilly, hesitating only once before uttering the lie.

'What did you do, state your problem and ask him to do the necessary?' he demanded, the anger in him unmistakable.

He was jealous, she realised—at first in amazement, then with the comfortless realisation that his jealousy was purely of the dog-in-the-manger variety. She was right about the size of his ego—he *had* wanted her, and his male ego was far too large for him to accept her having turned to another man.

'No, it was perfectly spontaneous,' she informed him with malicious relish. 'Something we both now realise should have happened...'

'Spare me the cloying romanticism of the details,' he murmured dismissively, reaching for his cup. The cup suddenly halted mid-way to his lips. 'I suppose it hasn't even occurred to you to consider your next problem,' he exclaimed, slamming down the cup.

'I'm sure you can't wait to tell me what this problem is,' she replied with sugary venom.

'Spontaneity such as you've been indulging in can lead to pregnancy—or didn't they teach you biology at ballet school?'

'I'm sorry to disappoint you, Jean-Luc,' she murmured, managing a smirk as she frantically racked her brains. 'But I'm not that stupid—I'm on the Pill.'

'Doesn't sound particularly spontaneous to me,' he retorted, his eyes narrowing over the rim of the cup he had once more raised.

'Actually, that's one of the things I wanted to explain,' she said quickly, almost gabbling in her haste to cover her lack of an answer to that last observation of his. 'Being on the Pill hasn't really agreed with me...it's made me extremely edgy...that's why I've been so unbearable recently. And I'd like to apologise for my unpleasant behaviour.'

'If the side-effects are so bad, shouldn't you stop taking it?' he enquired blandly.

'No...I...the doctor says it's something that often happens to begin with...my body will get used to it soon.'

'How very obliging of your body,' he murmured, stretching out once more on the sofa and returning Charlie to his chest—an action that managed to replace a whole volume of words in its eloquent message of dismissal.

CHAPTER SEVEN

'You're home early, Linda—everything OK?'

'Everything's fine—I'm just doing a spot of skiving,' grinned Linda, her eyes suddenly widening as they caught sight of what her sister was wearing. 'Jilly...you haven't been training?' she began nervously.

'A little,' murmured Jilly, flashing her a comforting smile. 'It's OK—this morning I took the bull by the horns and confronted one of the specialists at the hospital...'

'Jilly, you didn't mention you were going there today.'

'I hadn't an appointment or anything—but they did say if there was anything I wanted to ask—so today I asked...surprisingly enough, he seemed quite human, for a change.'

'And?' urged Linda impatiently.

'And...he pointed out to me that I'm not an invalid. That the problem with my hip was only a problem because of what the daily slog of being a dancer entailed...I can still use my body as a dancer, only not at full stretch.'

'Oh, Jilly,' choked Linda, her eyes suddenly filling.

'Oh, Jilly nothing!' retorted her sister. 'Full stretch, more often than not, meant pain, and I can't honestly say I miss it. So you're indulging in a spot of skiving, are you?' she added quickly, as she spotted the ominous trembling of her sister's lips.

'Me? I...oh, Jilly, you've been through so much...'

'Linda,' warned Jilly, taking her by the arms and practically forcing her on to a chair.

'Actually, I've had some rather good news,' managed Linda, battling against the threat of tears. 'The company wants me to freelance after the baby's born...I can't believe it! It's just what I wanted, but couldn't get up the nerve to ask for.'

'Give them some credit, love—they're not stupid,' chided Jilly. 'They realise how brilliant you are at your job and they want to keep you on any terms.'

'And that's your unbiased opinion, is it?' smiled Linda, a trifle tremulously.

'It is. And I think we ought to split open a pot of tea to celebrate such good news,' declared Jilly.

'Jilly, I meant to ask—how did last night go?' exclaimed Linda, as Jilly began filling the kettle.

Jilly felt a small shiver of apprehension ripple through her.

'Not too bad—but not too well, either...God knows what's wrong with him,' she muttered, trying with little success to mask the anxiety from her voice as she told Linda of the phone call and its effect on Jean-Luc.

'I can just imagine how completely unforthcoming he was when you tried quizzing him,' sighed Linda.

'A complete blank—though he was too upset to bother denying something was wrong,' replied Jilly unhappily. 'Needless to say, we ended up arguing. In a strange way, though, that probably wasn't such a bad thing...if it afforded him even a few moments' respite from whatever it is that troubles him so.'

They both gave a start as the doorbell began ringing with a shrill insistence.

'Really, do you have to...' Jilly's words of protest died on her lips as she flung open the door to find Jean-Luc standing there, Charlie in his arms and his finger still on the bell. 'Jean-Luc, must you...heavens, what's wrong with Charlie?' she shrieked, as the tabby looked up at her from one eye only. The other was closed and puffy, and there was blood matting its surrounding fur.

'I don't know—I've just got back and found him like this,' muttered Jean-Luc, at last removing his finger from the bell.

'It looks as though he's been fighting again,' sighed Jilly, quickly drawing back the hand she had stretched out to the cat as he growled warningly, and noticing several quite deep gashes on Jean-Luc's hands as she did so.

'Do you know the name of the vet my grandmother uses?'

Jilly frowned in concentration, then shook her head. 'No, but come in—perhaps Linda might know.'

'Heavens, what's happened to Charlie?' gasped Linda, as they entered the kitchen.

'Do you know which vet my grandmother uses?' demanded Jean-Luc, gazing down anxiously at the discontented bundle in his arms, and seemingly oblivious of the blood now dripping from one of the livid scratches on his hands.

'I know she always has a problem with vets,' mused Linda, her eyes widening at the sight of the blood and the cat hairs clinging to the immaculately tailored navy suit. 'Charlie tends to attack them and...'

'I know that!' interrupted Jean-Luc impatiently. 'But surely she gave you the name of someone who can cope with him.'

Linda shook her head. 'I'm afraid she didn't.' Her words were met with an exclamation of impatience from the man.

'We could try the Yellow Pages,' suggested Jilly.

'Good idea—I'll finish making the tea while you look,' replied Linda, casting an apprehensive glance towards the dark head now bending lovingly towards the cat. 'And I don't know about Charlie's eye, Jean-Luc, but he'll have yours out if you're not careful,' she added warningly.

'Jean-Luc, you sit down,' advised Jilly gently, taking the phone to the table and leafing through the directory. 'This one's quite near.' She began dialling.

'Ask for a house call,' ordered Jean-Luc. 'I can't find a travelling basket—and he'd only wreck a waiting-room.' He hoisted the cat up to his shoulder, murmuring softly to him in French.

'Hello—do you make house calls?' asked Jilly. 'A cat...no. Well, no—but he's not what you'd call completely tame...'

'If they won't come here—hang up,' growled Jean-Luc.

'Perhaps if you tried bathing his eye with a mild saline solution,' suggested Linda, as Jilly rang off for the third time.

Two pairs of blue eyes turned on her in hostile disbelief.

'Hell, I was only trying to be helpful,' she muttered indignantly, and carried on with making the tea.

'No—it's not terribly far from your surgery,' promised Jilly, flashing Jean-Luc a look of relief as she gave the address. 'Yes, it's Charlie!' she exclaimed. 'He knows him,' she whispered in an aside to Jean-Luc. 'I'm not sure...could you hold on a moment? He wants a few details,' she whispered, passing the receiver to Jean-Luc.

'No—I've not been able to see his eye—he won't open it...there's a lot of blood around it, though...thanks, I'd be most grateful.' He returned the receiver to Jilly, his face almost boyish in its relief. 'He'll be round in half an hour.'

'Thank heavens!' breathed Jilly, reaching out and stroking the large bundle straddling his shoulder.

'Don't irritate him!' exclaimed Jean-Luc sharply, drawing back from her hand.

'I wasn't irritating him...'

'For heaven's sake, you two!' giggled Linda weakly. 'And to think I used to accuse Lady Louise of pampering him!'

'How can you say we're pampering him?' demanded Jilly indignantly. 'You know Lady Lou would never forgive us if anything happened to him,' she added a trifle sheepishly.

Jean-Luc nodded, no trace of sheepishness on his handsome face as he carefully contorted his body to manoeuvre the teacup to his mouth without disturbing the cat.

At five to eight that evening, Jilly leapt to her feet.

'Time for Charlie's drops,' she announced, as Linda glanced up enquiringly from the book she was reading.

'If it takes two of you—and he's to have them every four hours—I suggest you move in next door,' she chuckled.

'We'll see how he is with this lot. With a bit of luck, the sedative the vet gave him will last the night—if it does, Jean-Luc should be able to cope on his own.'

She went straight up to Lady Lou's living-room after letting herself in.

Charlie was still curled up on the sofa, asleep, and Jean-Luc was sitting cross-legged on the floor, his back against the sofa, sheaves of paper on the coffee-table before him.

'*La petite garde-malade,*' he murmured, putting down the pen with which he had been writing and glancing up at her. 'The little nurse,' he translated, leaning over to switch off the alarm suddenly shrilling to life on the table. 'I'll hold him,' he announced, rising and passing Jilly the stoppered phial next to the clock. 'You insert the drops—two.'

'He looks so peaceful,' murmured Jilly, gazing down at the motionless cat.

'And let's hope that's how he stays,' muttered Jean-Luc, sitting down beside him. 'Are you ready?'

Jilly measured two drops into the dropper, then placed the bottle back on the table. She nodded.

With great tenderness, Jean-Luc lifted the cat on to his lap, holding him as the vet had instructed.

'He's certainly doped up,' murmured Jilly, quickly prising open the inflamed eye and inserting the drops.

The entire operation was over by the time Charlie got around to reacting with an indignant shake of his head and an uncharacteristically half-hearted growl.

'Now, go and wash your hands,' instructed Jean-Luc as he returned the cat to the sofa.

'Yes, sir,' replied Jilly, with a small salute, and immediately found her heart doing a reckless series of somersaults as he glanced up and smiled at her.

It was the ringing of the phone, as she entered the bathroom, that halted her frantic remonstrations with herself. It was a mixture of sixth sense and the fact that, as the night before, the phone had been given no chance to ring a second time, that made her prolong the washing of her hands for so inordinate a time. Then she reached out for a towel and began drying her hands, knowing it was sixth sense alone that now told her of his presence by the open door.

'Jilly, I'm afraid I have to go out.'

The terrible strain was back in his voice, she thought, her heart aching with anxiety as she turned and lifted reluctant eyes to his. And, as she felt the colour drain from her own face, she found herself wondering if any pallor could ever match the stark whiteness of his.

'Jean-Luc,' she whispered, her mouth dry from the nameless fear reaching out from him and into her. With a small, incoherent cry, the towel dropped from her hands, and suddenly she was beside him, her arms reaching out to encircle his unyielding body.

'I don't know how long I'll be,' he told her, his words bereft of all expression, his arms rigid by his sides.

'I'll be here for Charlie,' she whispered—and for you—she added silently.

'I know you will,' he answered hollowly, his dark head dropping to rest for a moment against hers before he gently disengaged her arms from around him. 'Perhaps I'll be back soon...' His words trailed to a halt as he turned from her—the words with which he had almost seemed to be attempting to inject some hope into himself.

'Charlie, I'm almost beginning to hate you!' wailed Jilly tearfully, as she received yet another vicious sideswipe from unsheathed claws.

The midnight session had been bad enough, she thought wearily, but now the sedative had worn off completely and the hissing bundle of malevolence now confronting her was making it perfectly—not to mention painfully—clear that he had no intention of letting the dropper anywhere near him.

'Charlie, it's for your own good,' she pleaded, gazing down helplessly at the large tear in her nightgown which might easily have been her own flesh.

She would be mad to try again, with him in this mood, she warned herself, sighing defeatedly as she returned the dropper to the bottle.

'OK—you win,' she said, with another sigh. 'Charlie—come back!' she groaned, as the cat thudded off the sofa and stalked angrily towards the door. She rose, her heart suddenly thudding as she heard a soft tread on the stairs.

'Jean-Luc . . . oh, thank heavens it's you!' she gasped, sinking back on to the sofa in relief as he appeared in the doorway.

'I didn't frighten you, did I?' he asked quietly.

'No...I...' She shrugged, her eyes searching the dark shadows of beard on his face—so dark it had the appearance of several days' growth. But at least much of the tension seemed to have gone from him, she thought, relieved.

He stooped down and picked up Charlie, his eyes seeming to soften in the dimness of the light as they skimmed over the slight, dishevelled figure perched on the edge of the sofa.

'I see he's been giving you a rough time of it,' he observed softly.

Jilly nodded, suddenly inordinately conscious of the flimsy cotton of her nightgown and wondering what had possessed her to dress for bed—she had had no sleep. She nervously began smoothing her hands over the jagged tear by her left knee.

'It took me almost half an hour to get the midnight lot in—now he won't let me near him.'

'Jilly, you shouldn't even have attempted it,' he exclaimed, returning Charlie to the floor and coming to sit next to her.

'I soon gave up,' she muttered, wondering if the unevenness of her breathing was as obvious to him as it was to her as he reached out and gently traced a livid scratch on her arm.

'Not soon enough,' he sighed. 'Jilly, Charlie can be lethal...'

'I'm all right,' she blurted out, moving her arm away from the seductive gentleness of his probing fingers. 'But you—is everything all right with you?' she asked, appalled to hear how awkward her words sounded.

'Yes—everything's all right with me,' he echoed gently.

'I'm glad.'

'I'll be in a position to explain soon...'

'You don't have to explain anything to me,' blurted out Jilly, her eyes concentrating on the dark-suited legs next to her, wondering if she should try calming herself by counting the scores of cat hairs still clinging to them.

'Don't I?'

'No—you don't,' she whispered, a small shiver rippling through her as his fingers reached out and gently stroked her cheek.

'You're cold, Jilly.'

'No...I...I forgot to bring my dressing-gown round with me when I went for my things—actually I don't know why I bothered to get into my night things, I...' Her words petered to a halt.

As she had been gabbling away, he had slipped out of his jacket and was now draping it round her shoulders.

It was like being in his arms, she thought miserably, as the warmth and fragrance of his body seemed to envelop hers.

'Perhaps we ought to see about getting this monster dealt with,' he murmured, reaching down and lifting the cat which had flopped down by his feet.

Jilly nodded, her hand automatically reaching out for the drops.

'My, Charlie—you're well and truly in her bad books,' he chuckled to the cat. 'I wasn't even ticked off for referring to you as a monster.'

'And what happened to this relationship you two allegedly have—based on mutual indifference?' murmured Jilly as, with scarcely a flicker of protest, the cat allowed her to administer the drops.

'We feel it spoils our macho images to admit to anything more,' chuckled Jean-Luc, lazily stroking his docile burden. 'Come along, Charles, off you get,' he ordered, returning the cat to his place on the floor. 'We have to see about getting Jilly tucked up.'

'I might as well go next door... unless you'll need me for the eight o'clock dose,' she added hesitantly. 'But anyway, none of the other beds is made up...'

'You're not traipsing next door at this hour. Have my bed—I'm quite capable of making up another for myself.'

'But...'

'Jilly, you're not going to argue, are you?' he chided, slipping his jacket from around her. 'You know I'm much bigger than you are, and you know how easily I dealt with Charlie,' he laughed, rising and sweeping her up into his arms.

At first it was the unexpected shock of his action that brought her arms to cling tightly round his neck.

But then it was the languorous excitement seeping through her that kept them there—as though round him were the only place they should be.

'Jilly, you're throttling me,' he whispered huskily, as he elbowed open the bedroom door.

'I'm sorry,' she croaked, startled to find her arms refusing to ease their hold. 'You almost have a beard,' she added, scarcely recognising those breathlessly expelled words as her own as she felt the tingling rasp of his cheek against hers.

'Have I?' he breathed, his voice as distorted as hers as he rested one knee on the bed as though to lower her.

'Yes.' Not only were her arms refusing to release him, but her cheek remained pressed against the roughness of his.

'Jilly... when I picked you up just now, there was no thought in my mind other than to make sure you got some sleep.'

'And now?' She shivered as his arms gently eased her till she was kneeling on the bed, their bodies almost touching.

'And now,' he groaned softly, his hands sliding down from her waist to caress the gentle swell of her hips. 'And now... Jilly, now I'm beginning to feel...'

'Devastated?' she whispered, the word catching in her throat as a tense, expectant excitement took possession of her.

'Totally devastated,' he groaned as he pulled her against him, his lips harsh in their impatience as they found and parted hers.

'Jilly, this isn't advisable,' he breathed, as she melted against him. 'I'm not in the least sure that I know what I'm doing.'

Yet his hands knew exactly what they were doing, as they freed her trembling body from the nightgown. And his lips also knew, as they burned their impassioned trail down her throat to begin a softly panting exploration of breasts that swelled and tautened beneath his touch.

With a soft groan, he took her hands and guided them to the buttons of his shirt, and her fingers obeyed unquestioningly, her body answering the shudders of excitement rippling through his as she removed the shirt from him. She felt a strange wildness possess her as her lips and fingers explored his naked torso, delighting in the smooth firmness of muscle beneath them and the softly springing sensation of the hairs matting his chest.

And when he tried to disengage himself from her twining arms, she could only shake her head, clinging in the fierce possessiveness of an ardour she had no means to control.

'You'll have to let go if I'm to finish undressing,' he protested hoarsely, his attempt at teasing laughter becoming a ragged gasp as his mouth returned to hers, clinging and plundering with a mounting wildness as his hands swept impatiently down the length of her body, pressing and moulding her to him even as he attempted to move away.

'Get under the cover,' he pleaded huskily, forcing her pliant body back as he leaned over and drew back the duvet.

As though in a daze, Jilly did as he bade; part of her crying out for the touch of him for which her body now burned, while another part of her seemed to step aside, almost recoiling from the savage need threatening to overwhelm her. And that other part of her detected a fear mingling with the myriad of alien emotions raging within her, darting back and forth in her consciousness as that tall figure was suddenly starkly outlined in the shadowy semi-darkness before stooping to draw back the quilt and join her.

She felt the movement of his body next to hers, that same strange mixture of fear and longing beginning to rack her body with an uncontrollable trembling as he lay beside her, making no move to touch her—no movement at all.

There were things she should be doing, she thought in panic as fear suddenly became predominant—and she had no idea what they were. She was going to have to explain to him...explain her fear, her complete ignorance...

'Jean-Luc!' she blurted out, turning towards him even as he moved as though in response to her cry.

And then she was in his arms, clinging to him with no memory of the words she had been about to utter as the naked power of his aroused body awoke a primitive, irresistible need in her that superseded all fear.

'You were afraid,' he whispered huskily, his hands cupping the breasts his mouth lowered to caress as she trembled against him.

'No,' she denied softly, no lie in that denial as her fingers entwined possessively in the thickness of his hair and her body became possessed of a rhythm of its own—curving to his with a wildness of abandon that resisted his sudden efforts to restrain.

'Oh, Jilly, you should feel afraid...to be wanted as I want you,' he groaned, his lips and his hands goading her to ignore his attempts to hold her back as the longing within her swelled to an unbearable need.

'Jean-Luc...please,' she pleaded wildly, her touch feverish in its demands as her legs began entwining around his.

Then his name became a chanted sob on her lips as his legs stilled the impatience of hers, guiding them as her fingers raked the length of his back and brought a groaned shudder from him.

'Oh, my impatient Jilly,' he cried out, his mouth a moist bringer of torment and ecstasy as it opened against her breast to bring wild cries of longing from her as his tongue teased against her engorged nipple.

'Jean-Luc,' she sobbed. 'I...' Her words choked to a gasped halt as he cried out her name and brought his body fully over hers, stilling her with the sudden poised tension within him that for one instant of hesitation resurrected the ghost of fear within her, before her body was accepting and welcoming the sweet plunder of his. It was as she felt the unrestrained wildness within her reach out and capture him that the barriers of the unknown crumbled within her, tumbling free an ecstasy that was a shivering, exploding madness of pleasure—a madness that tossed her from one exquisite sensation to the next—a madness that defied all reason in its magical ability time and again to improve on perfection.

And when she was convinced there could be no more, the words began tumbling from his lips, soft, wild words she didn't understand but which seemed to have the power to describe the ecstasy with which he filled her. And it was those abandoned cries and the frenzied guidance of his body that showed her there was yet more, carrying her in sobbing acquiescence over and beyond the boundaries of perfection, till they could only tumble from the explosive pinnacles of sensation into the blissful lethargy of fulfilment.

'How could I have even dreamt anything could ever be like that?' she choked uncertainly, her hands softly caressing the body still shuddering in the aftermath of passion in her arms.

'How could you indeed, Jilly,' he murmured, leaving her no time to ponder the oddly non-committal tone of his words as he rolled over on to his back, carrying her body with his.

'Jean-Luc?' she murmured, luxuriating in the heavy thud of his heartbeat beneath her and delighting in the salty moisture of his skin as her lips played against the curve of his neck.

'Jilly?' Her name was almost a sigh and there was a stillness in the arms that held her—a stillness that was almost impersonal when compared with the fierce ardour with which they had embraced her only moments before.

'There are so many things jumbled around inside me— so many things I could say.' The words had slipped out without thought, and to Jilly's critical ears they sounded only banal.

'Such as?'

Such as the sudden sadness now penetrating her drowsy haze of contentment. A sadness for the love which filled her and which, even as it had been given total expression in the physical act of loving, had not dared express itself in words. Such as the many emotions centred around love which were now burrowing secretively inside her for fear their expression might bring rebuff from the man in whose disconcertingly passive arms she now lay.

'Don't fret, my Jilly,' he whispered after a long silence, cupping her face in his hands and raising it till she was gazing down at the shadowy outline of his features, barely discernible in the shadowy half-light. 'I shan't pry,' he murmured, drawing her down to a kiss in which sadness mingled with sweetness.

He had called her his Jilly...and perhaps she was only imagining the sadness, she told herself, as he drew down her head to nestle once more against his shoulder.

At eight o'clock the shrill nagging of the alarm clock summoned them to treat the now vilely cantankerous Charlie.

After their initial dazed scramble to fling on dressing-gowns, came an odd moment between them that was awkward, almost constrained. But it was a moment that came and went before Jilly could pause to examine it as they stalked their enraged quarry through the house and were both treated to vicious reprisals for their loving ministrations.

'Thank God the midday dose is the last!' groaned Jean-Luc, flopping prone on to his back on the floor of his grandmother's bedroom where they had at last succeeded in catching Charlie.

Kneeling beside him, Jilly gave a heartfelt nod of agreement as she returned the dropper to its bottle and screwed it tightly.

'Did he bite you badly?' she asked, suddenly remembering that fleeting moment of constraint and trying to keep its return at bay.

'I could be in danger of losing a finger—or two,' he murmured, his tone softly teasing as he removed the phial from her hands. 'Though there is that well-known remedy you could try in an attempt to save them.'

Jilly's eyes rose, vivid memories sending a shiver of excitement coursing through her as she met his lazy smile.

'And what exactly is this well-known remedy?' she asked, her words distorted by her sudden breathlessness.

Gazing at her with a theatrical expression of pity mingled with disbelief, he held out his hand to her. 'Kissing it better, of course. My God, Jilly, we'll have to start doing something about these gaping blanks in your education.'

Though her own hands were now trembling with a severity she felt he couldn't fail to notice, she took his hand in hers, bending down to kiss the fingers one by one.

'I think you're supposed to have your patient tucked up in bed before you begin treatment,' he observed, leaning back on his free arm and gazing up at her with a look that was blatant in its seduction. 'Do you think you can manage to carry me down the stairs?'

'No problem,' she grinned, happiness exploding within her as she placed one arm round his back and the other under his knees. All that moved, when she gave a heave, were her arms.

'Big and brawny though you are—you might drop me,' he chuckled, ducking suddenly and hoisting her over his shoulder as he stood up.

'And you're going to drop me! Jean-Luc!' she shrieked, as he descended the stairs to the first floor.

'O, ye of little faith,' he admonished, flinging her in a heap on the bed. 'You'd better start counting fingers,' he added, throwing himself down beside her and dangling his hand under her nose. 'I think I might have lost one on the way down.'

Jilly gave his hand a thorough examination, once again kissing each finger.

'All present and correct,' she murmured, finding the words extremely difficult to enunciate because of the suffocating pounding of her heart. 'But just to be on the safe side, perhaps I ought to count them again...shall I?'

He shook his head, the eyes now holding hers darkening almost to the navy of his dressing-gown as his hands undid the belt of her robe.

'Kiss me, Jilly,' he whispered huskily, as his hands began moving against her skin, bringing an involuntary gasp of longing from her with the tormenting lightness of their touch. 'Kiss me and tell me I'm not dreaming.'

The delicate sureness of his hands awoke a savage longing in her as he drew her down to the mouth that opened hungrily to the soft welcome of hers.

'Tell me the magic between us wasn't just a dream,' he groaned urgently against her pliant mouth.

'How can I tell you that?' she breathed huskily. 'When it could only have been a beautiful, magical dream.'

'But can such a dream be repeated—shared again, Jilly?' he demanded hoarsely, sliding the robe from around her and slipping free of his before his arms reached out for her.

'It can,' she cried out wildly as his arms crushed her to him and her body gave instant response to the savage message of desire in his.

And they found again that explosive magic which might have been a dream, recreating the wild enchantment of the spell each cast on the other, learning that between them they had the power to create the magic of pure ecstasy.

Yet it was a power so devastating that it brought with it an element of fear, when later Jilly found herself questioning whether it might not have been better for her never to have experienced such enchantment if it were something she was one day to be denied.

CHAPTER EIGHT

'You're a fine one to accuse me of being childish, Jean-Luc,' protested Jilly, her eyes sparkling not with anger but with an overwhelming surfeit of happiness that allowed no room for the doubts and uncertainties now languishing in the furthest recesses of her mind. 'Why won't you tell me where we're going?'

'I've already explained—my lips are sealed by others,' he murmured with infuriating mystery, the hand holding hers, as it had ever since they had left the car, tightening momentarily.

'What others?' demanded Jilly, hesitating fractionally as they entered through the plate-glass doors of a building that had an oddly familiar feel to it, even though she knew she had never been here before.

'Actually—an other,' he replied unhelpfully, tugging her towards the reception desk.

'Dr de Sauvignet,' greeted the receptionist, smiling in recognition.

'We're expected,' stated Jean-Luc, and immediately cut through the words the girl began uttering. 'We'll go straight up.'

'Jean-Luc!' exclaimed Jilly suddenly, as she was led into a nearby lift. 'This is a hospital, isn't it? One of those extortionately expensive places where all the celebrities...'

'Jilly,' he growled warningly.

'Jean-Luc—why are we here?' she demanded apprehensively as the lift doors swung open.

'You'll see, but a word of warning,' he cautioned, his face serious as he turned and looked down at her. 'I don't want any remarks about the social injustice of some people being able to afford treatment in a place like this...I've already had it up to my eyeballs...'

'Oh, my God!' croaked Jilly, her knees suddenly buckling. 'Lady Lou! Your grandmother's in here!' she accused as a firm arm caught and steadied her. 'Jean-Luc...'

'Jilly, she's all right—I swear it. You might as well hear it from her,' he added, opening one of the doors a few paces down the corridor.

Tearing free of his restraining arm, Jilly hurled herself into the room, then gave a choked gasp at the sight of the familiar figure propped up on pillows in the bed before her.

'What happened to you?' she cried, her words barely coherent as she took stumbling steps towards the bed.

'It's quite a long story,' chuckled the old lady who, it suddenly struck Jilly with a force like a physical blow, had come to mean more to her than her own mother.

'Why didn't you tell me she was in hospital?' accused Jilly, rounding on Jean-Luc in her fear and confusion.

'You mustn't blame my poor boy,' chided Lady Louise, patting the bed invitingly. 'Now, come along and sit down—both of you.'

Jilly sat down, trembling with shock.

'Would it be all right if I gave you a hug?' she asked querulously, then flung herself into the arms that opened to her. 'Are you really all right? What happened?' she sobbed, appalled by the way she was going to pieces as she felt not only Lady Louise's hands but also Jean-Luc's pat her consolingly. 'I'm sorry I'm behaving like this...Lady Lou, did you have an accident in Jamaica?' she choked, scrubbing away the tears streaming down her cheeks and trying desperately to get a grip on herself as she felt Jean-Luc gently draw her back till she was leaning against his solid body.

'I never went to Jamaica, darling,' sighed Lady Louise. 'I've been incarcerated in this over-priced dump for over-privileged...'

'*Grand-mère*,' groaned Jean-Luc in laughing protest, dropping his chin to Jilly's shoulder. 'Jilly, she wouldn't let me tell anyone. My own mother didn't even know till I rang her—and then my uncle—last night.'

'Didn't know what?' exclaimed Jilly.

'That my infuriating darling of a grandmother was now paying the price of having buried her head in the sand for the best part of a year. First of all she chose to ignore the warning symptoms her body was giving her. Then she put two and two together and came up with five—if not six—and decided to sit back and await meeting up with Grandpa Henry...which she had become convinced would be any day.'

'Stop exaggerating, darling,' murmured Lady Louise. 'I had a little turn in the street a few weeks ago...'

'A lucky little turn,' snorted Jean-Luc indignantly. 'Because the doctor who saw her ordered her into hospital for a thorough going-over!'

Jilly turned in an attempt to see his face, and found her lips almost touching his cheek.

'Jean-Luc, you must have been worried out of your mind,' she whispered, conscious of the colour suddenly warming her cheeks as she turned her face away from his disturbing proximity. 'Lady Lou, why wouldn't you let him tell me?'

'Perhaps I wasn't fair on my boy,' sighed the old lady, reaching out to ruffle the dark head at Jilly's shoulder.

'But I'd have thought you'd be the first to understand why,' she added, moving her hand from her grandson's head to Jilly's cheek and stroking it gently, 'considering how determinedly you were hiding your own problems from everyone. You weren't as successful as I was—but you tried to keep them all to yourself, didn't you, my little Jilly?' she chided.

'I'd have told you,' muttered Jilly guiltily.

'Perhaps, but I was most relieved to learn you'd mistaken Jean-Luc for a medical doctor,' sighed Lady Louise. 'Otherwise I'm not sure what I'd have done... having to abandon you when you so desperately needed someone. How lucky we both were to have my beautiful boy to confide in,' she added with a chuckle.

'And both of you confided with such refreshing spontaneity,' drawled Jean-Luc sarcastically.

'Of course we did,' murmured his grandmother innocently. 'There's something so dependable about a mathematician—did you get your paper finished, darling?'

'I've finished it,' he retorted drily. 'Though I can't imagine any other treatise having been written under such traumatic conditions.'

'Which brings me to Charlie,' stated Lady Louise sharply, startling them both. 'Jean-Luc, why don't you wander off and try to rustle us up some tea, while I cross-examine Jilly?' she added briskly.

Jilly was conscious of the sudden tensing of the body that straightened behind hers. Then she felt his hands descend lightly on her shoulders to give them a warning squeeze.

'What do you want to know about Charlie?' he asked casually.

'You can stop the morse code on Jilly's shoulders,' Lady Louise informed him tartly. 'I may have been groggy last night, but even I couldn't miss the fact that you were covered in Charlie fur... and the pair of you are also covered in scratches.'

'Proper little Sherlock Holmes you're turning into,' chuckled Jean-Luc resignedly, rising from the bed. 'Charlie's OK, I promise you... and I dare say Jilly and I will recover, just in case you're interested.'

'I don't know what was in the drops, but they were miraculous,' said Jilly, as she finished her story. 'We gave him the last lot at midday and his eye's fully opened now—still a bit bloodshot, but in a much better state than poor Jean-Luc's hands.'

'Ah, my beautiful grandson,' murmured Lady Louise slyly.

Jilly lowered her head as she felt the colour rushing to her cheeks.

'I remember the first time I met his father... I was so afraid for my daughter, Julia. You see, the de Sauvignet men have always been renowned for being beautiful, charming heart-breakers—and my Julia was so passionately in love,' she sighed. 'But the de Sauvignet men never deserved the reputation of callousness often attributed to them. It was just that they all have that same vein of almost brutal honesty in them—a directness that would never let them cheat women by vowing a love they didn't feel. A de Sauvignet man deals only in the truth, and God help those who forget that. Which was why, when Dominic de Sauvignet told Henry and me he loved Julia, all our fears disappeared. That reminds me,' she chuckled. 'The lovebirds—which they still are—insist I go over to France to stay with them when I'm let out of here...do you think you could stomach Charlie Miles for a couple of weeks more?'

'You know you don't even have to ask,' laughed Jilly, hugging her.

'There's one question I wouldn't ask...though I think I already have the answer,' stated Lady Louise quietly, cupping Jilly's face in her hands and gazing anxiously into her eyes. 'Being a typical de Sauvignet, Jean-Luc resented the deception my being here has involved him in. Perhaps we were both foolish keeping our fears bottled up...and perhaps the de Sauvignets are right...that only total honesty is the best policy in the long run.'

Jilly found her gaze held in the faded blue of an infinite tenderness and something told her that, in her own roundabout way, her elderly friend had offered words of warning.

'I remember hearing tell of Louis-Jacques de Sauvignet when I was a girl,' reminisced Lady Louise, her hands dropping from Jilly's face. 'Now, he must have been Jean-Luc's great-uncle, or was it his...' She broke off as the door opened. 'Jean-Luc, was Louis-Jacques your great-uncle, or...'

'Grandfather, actually,' grinned Jean-Luc. 'But enough of my ancestors—Jilly and I have our marching orders. Your surgeon, *Grand-mère*, is on his way to examine his handiwork.'

'And pretty poor handiwork it is, too,' grumbled Lady Louise ungratefully. 'The man's merely tacked me up—using an upholstery needle, by the feel of it.'

Jilly immediately began bombarding Jean-Luc with questions as they left the hospital.

'There's a coffee-shop round the corner,' he told her, grabbing her by the hand. 'And I don't intend answering a single question till I've at least one coffee—more likely two—in me. I'm almost dead on my feet.' He gave a low, rumbling chuckle as he drew her arm round him and slipped his across her shoulder. 'Mind you, you can't be feeling much better,' he murmured softly, his lips caressing against her temple.

With a small sigh of utter contentment, Jilly let her head drop against him as they strolled down the street. And she gave up trying to examine the happiness careering out of control inside her and gave in to the bliss of wallowing in it.

She had let her imagination run away with her, she told herself contentedly, by thinking he could be falling in love with Linda. No man in love with another woman could possibly have made love with the unbridled intensity he had shown towards her. Perhaps there had been no actual words of love between them... but what they had shared could only have stemmed from love.

And even though he infuriatingly insisted on downing a coffee before uttering a single word to her in the coffee-house, there was a softness in the eyes that caressed hers all the while he drank—a softness that seemed indistinguishable from love.

'OK—here we go,' he grinned, refilling his cup. 'Originally, my grandmother's problem was put down to a fairly mundane intestinal blockage—I was given to understand she'd be in and out within the week.' His lips tightened with sudden memory. 'But nothing turned out to be in the least mundane. She ended up having two exploratory bouts of surgery before they could make an accurate diagnosis... and even then, it wasn't until after yesterday's operation that they could be sure that all would be well.'

'And it definitely is?' demanded Jilly anxiously, fearing he might have kept something from her.

'One hundred per cent now, thank God,' he sighed, his heartfelt relief dispelling her fears.

'But why did she tell you?' puzzled Jilly. 'Why not your mother?'

'She didn't intend telling anyone. I happened to ring her to tell her I needed some peace and quiet to finish a paper I'd been writing, and as my intended visit happen to coincide with her going into hospital, she had no option but to tell me the truth.' He chuckled. 'You see, she knew I'd never swallow her story about going back to Jamaica...'

'Because you knew she wouldn't go back there without Henry Miles,' exclaimed Jilly, then immediately clapped her hand over her mouth as he began laughing softly at her familiar reference to his grandfather.

'I've got so used to hearing her refer to him like that,' she muttered in embarrassment.

'It's the way we've all got used to referring to him,' he acknowledged gently. 'Jilly, she's been very worried about you...'

'I do wish she hadn't,' groaned Jilly guiltily. 'She had enough on her plate as it was.'

'She loves you, Jilly. She was bound to worry,' he pointed out quietly. 'And I was wrong to be so hard on you. Your life was disintegrating around you...my grandmother got very cross with me. She kept saying I could never understand unless I had actually seen you dance,' he sighed.

'Is that why you came to classes with me?' she asked shyly, a strange warmth prickling its way through her.

He nodded.

'But that couldn't give you much idea what I was like when I really danced.'

'As my grandmother was very quick to point out,' he murmured ruefully. 'She's ordered a video of you dancing in *Don Quixote*—I've been instructed to sit through it when it arrives and then make my judgement.'

Jilly pulled a small face. 'You don't have to do that,' she protested. 'Anyway, why hark back to the past? I've the future to sort out.'

His eyes were serious as they met hers. 'You once started telling me you planned furthering your education.'

Jilly nodded, telling him of Justin's feelings about her gifts as a physiotherapist.

'Unfortunately I need A-levels to study it—but I'm determined to get them,' she added.

'And Justin?' he asked, his voice very quiet.

Jilly felt her heart skip several beats and her head suddenly rang with Lady Louise's words—her warning that it didn't pay to be dishonest with a de Sauvignet man.

'Jean-Luc...I lied about Justin...he and I were never lovers,' she stammered.

It frightened her how suddenly his eyes could change—moments before filled with a softness she had almost fooled herself into thinking might be love; now cold and withdrawn.

'I don't know why I lied...' Her words petered to nothing. The realisation that she was having to resort to yet another lie in trying to undo the first appalled her. 'I thought you'd have realised...known...'

'That I was making love to a virgin?' he asked coldly. 'It isn't always possible to tell.'

Even the memory of the happiness to which she had so foolishly clung earlier was stripped from her with the icy blast of his words.

'There's one thing that bothers me, Jilly,' he stated, in that same chilling tone. 'You are—as you claimed to be—on the Pill?'

'No,' she whispered hoarsely, her hands clenching and unclenching in her lap.

'I like to think I would have found the strength of will not to have made love to you, had I known that,' he rasped. 'As I seem to remember pointing out to you once before, lovemaking is an act of procreation...doesn't that fact trouble you in the least?'

She was worse than merely childish—as he had so frequently accused her—she was totally irresponsible, she told herself, sickened by the realization.

'And that brings me to another intriguing question,' he stated, giving up waiting for her to reply. 'If your strange behaviour wasn't caused by your being on the pill—what exactly did cause it?'

Even before she began speaking, Jilly knew with a premonition that bordered on conviction that she was about to damn herself irrevocably in his eyes. Lady Lou could never have envisaged this, she thought numbly, when she had spoken about honesty being the best policy in the long run. And now she was facing the de Sauvignet man she loved and having to explain the lies he so despised.

'You thought I was trying to curry favour with Linda—a married, not to mention pregnant, woman—merely because I showed concern over you?' he demanded with venomous outrage.

'I realise now that your concern took your mind off your grandmother.'

'Do you really!' he exclaimed angrily. 'Do you honestly think that's the way my mind works? Though perhaps, in some small way, you're right,' he conceded abruptly, his hand shaking visibly as he brought the cup to his lips. Suddenly the cup was slammed back into its saucer, without ever reaching his lips. '*Nom de Dieu!* I've always admitted to having problems understanding you—but you've obviously made no attempt whatsoever to understand who or what I am! To you I'm a philanderer who snubbed you in favour of her sister.' He rose, flinging a note on the table. 'We're going,' he told her abruptly.

'You may be going—I'm not,' retorted Jilly through pale and numbed lips.

'This place may be virtually empty—but even now we have quite an audience,' he informed her with threatening softness.

Jilly automatically glanced round and saw several waitresses hanging on their every word.

'If you wish, we can finish our discussion here,' he continued.

A discussion it certainly was not, thought Jilly, still mentally reeling from the explosive fury of his reaction. But it was the thought of what it might well deteriorate into that brought her to her feet.

'Jean-Luc, please try to understand,' she began as he started up the car.

'When I said we'd finish the discussion elsewhere, I didn't mean while I was driving,' he informed her harshly, terrifying her with the speed with which he hurled the car into the traffic.

'And you can open your eyes,' he snarled, as she sat with her eyes tightly shut. 'I may feel like killing you, but I don't happen to feel suicidal.'

She opened her eyes, not from any wish to obey, but in the irrational hope that physical fear might distract her from the savage sense of loss and hopelessness now spreading its way throughout her.

By the time he brought the car to a screeching halt before the houses, she knew she could take no more.

He had asked for the truth and she had given him it, she told herself with empty weariness as she struggled from the seat-belt and fumbled with the door-catch.

'Where do you think you're going?' he demanded, leaning across her and slamming shut the door her numbed hands had just managed to open.

'Just leave me alone,' she choked, now finding herself battling against tears she would have rather died than allow to fall. 'My thinking was muddled and wrong and unforgivable... but it doesn't alter the fact that those were my thoughts at the time. I didn't consciously judge or blame you...'

'Jilly, I'm not interested in what was going on in that warped mind of yours,' he cut in coldly. 'Though I'd like an explanation of just one thing—your eagerness to jump into my bed. Was it—as you so glibly claimed— merely in order to shed your virginity? Or did you have some foolish idea you were luring me from your sister with your womanly charms?'

He had asked for the truth and she had given it, she thought numbly...but not the final truth. That she could never give him, she realised with sickening finality as her eyes rose to his and recoiled from the bitter disgust chilling their blue depths.

'It was probably a bit of both,' she stated, feeling the capacity for ever knowing joy again dying in her as she turned and clambered through the door which he had so pointedly leaned over to open for her. 'And I suppose you might as well hear it all—there was even a time when I suspected you might be responsible for my losing the role I was to dance in *Swan Lake*!'

CHAPTER NINE

JILLY paused in her task of emptying the dishwasher, disturbed to find she was counting yet again. Counting spoons, counting saucers; adding these sums to the totals of the glasses and cups she had removed from the dishwasher—counting, because filling her head with these endless numbers was the only means her mind had found to keep at bay the destructive army of thoughts massing within it.

The flimsy protection afforded her by that mindless ritual of counting was stripped from her by the sudden ringing of the doorbell.

'I'll get it,' called Linda, as Jilly found herself gasping for breath.

This is ridiculous, she berated herself harshly—this nerve-shattering alert her body jangled into each time there was a ring at the door. Another day like the past one and she would be a neurotic wreck.

'It's a bit unexpected, isn't it, Jean-Luc?'

As Linda's voice drifted in from the hallway, Jilly was forcing herself to take deep, steadying breaths.

'A little,' murmured the voice that had the power to destroy any semblance of control within her. 'Mainly because I seem to have lost track of time.'

'Jilly, Jean-Luc tells me he's going back to Paris today,' exclaimed Linda, as she and Jean-Luc entered the kitchen.

'Is he?' managed Jilly, her back to them as she slowly began lifting plates from the dishwasher, numbers still dancing in random confusion in her mind.

'The paper I was writing has to be with the publishers by tomorrow,' stated Jean-Luc.

'What about Lady Lou?' asked Jilly, her words tumbling into the silence her agitated mind felt was becoming unnaturally prolonged.

'She's coming out on Friday—my mother will be over to take her back to France with her.'

He sounded so relaxed, so completely normal, noticed Jilly, while fighting to check the feeling that was almost panic threatening her.

'She'll be round to collect some of my grandmother's things on Friday morning.'

'Isn't Lady Lou coming back here before going to France?' asked Jilly, closing the cupboard in which she had stacked the plates. Her head moved a fraction, and he was in her line of vision, his eyes not on her as he lowered himself on to a chair.

Even before his eyes rose to meet hers, the memories were flooding into her mind, almost crushing her with their vivid sensuality in that instant before their eyes met. Through the coolness of the blue that was now levelled at her lurched the memory of the languorous seduction with which those same eyes had once beckoned hers.

'No—she's got it into her head it might upset Charlie if she appears then takes off again.'

'I suppose she's right,' said Jilly, surprised she was capable of words so mundane while her senses remained caught in the torrid trap of memories.

Yet it was as though there was no memory in him— of a passion so devastating that even its haunting memory was a vivid torment.

'Jean-Luc, have you time for a coffee?' asked Linda, anxiety creeping into the eyes that flickered from her tense and pale sister to the guarded neutrality on the face of the man seated beside her. Her eyes narrowed as she caught his almost imperceptible hesitation before answering.

'No—I'd best be on my way,' he said quietly, his eyes lifting once again to Jilly's. 'I'd like to have a word with you...if you wouldn't mind, Jilly.'

'Jilly can see you out,' announced Linda, rising. 'I'm dying for a coffee...can't stomach it in the mornings, at the moment, but after midday I seem to crave one.'

'Jilly?' murmured Jean-Luc, rising also.

Jilly nodded, conscious of the brittle constraint chilling the air around them.

'Well...goodbye, Linda,' he said softly, taking Linda by the shoulders and kissing both her cheeks before gazing affectionately down at her. 'Take care of the little one.'

'I shall,' murmured Linda, giving him a sudden hug. 'And thanks for everything.'

'Don't say that,' he teased. 'I still get the odd twinge of guilt over that wretched advertising dream of yours.'

'If ever you have a brainstorm and change your mind...'

'You'd be the first to hear,' he chuckled softly. 'But happy hunting, anyway...I'm sure you'll find him. Jilly?'

Jilly followed him, her eyes clinging to the tall figure ahead of her—drinking in each fluid movement of that graceful body, as though accepting this could be their last ever glimpse of him.

'Are you all right?' he asked abruptly, his tone devoid of the concern he voiced as he opened the door.

'Yes...I'm all right,' she lied, pride willing her to retain some dignity in these their last moments.

'You say it with such ease,' he accused, his face grim. 'I've left my Paris telephone number on my grandmother's bureau. If it turns out that you're pregnant—ring me.'

'I'm not pregnant,' she stated tonelessly. 'I found out this morning.'

She heard his sharp intake of breath as she tried to stifle that part of her crying out to know what his reaction would have been had she been pregnant.

'How am I to know you're not lying?' he demanded, tilting his head sideways till it rested against the door, then momentarily closing his eyes.

'I suppose you're not to know,' replied Jilly in that same utterly toneless voice. 'But why should I lie about something like that?'

The words came, but were no part of her. Everything that was in her ached to reach out to him—to hold him—to be held once more in his arms.

'No, I suppose you'd have no reason to lie about something like that,' he echoed hollowly, straightening. 'So...you'll take good care of Charlie, won't you?' he finished, an unfamiliar uncertainty in his tone.

Jilly nodded, no longer able to trust herself to speak.

Then his hand reached out—almost as though he were about to touch her cheek. His fingers suddenly clenched—their movement abruptly checked—then his hand dropped once more to his side.

'*Adieu*, Jilly.'

He closed the door behind him, a solid sound that contained no anger. *Adieu*.

Not so long ago, she had opened that same door, never realising it had been the symbolic opening of her heart.

And now he had closed that door, never knowing he took with him a love that clung to him alone, which without him could only wither and die.

'Jilly, I've put on the coffee—come and have some.'

Linda's voice seemed to come from so far away, yet there was a gentle pressure on her shoulders that guided her from the spot to which she felt rooted.

'Jilly?' There was a softly pleading sadness in Linda's voice.

'I was thinking... I'm going to see the ballet director tomorrow,' said Jilly suddenly, the words gushing from her as though to sweep away the savage pain awakening inside her. 'Justin's right, I have a flair... the others always used to come to me to sort out their minor twinges. But the director will have some ideas exactly how I should channel that flair... I'm not stupid. I *could* get A-levels if I needed them—I'd work. Justin says there are schools called crammers, where...'

'Jilly! Stop it! Please, darling,' choked Linda, hugging her with a protective fierceness.

'And I'm going to look after you, Linda,' gabbled Jilly blindly. 'I know David's due back soon, but...'

'Jilly, I can't bear to see you like this... what in God's name has he done to you?' choked Linda.

'Don't blame Jean-Luc,' said Jilly quietly, that sudden, almost manic spate of words spent as rapidly as it had erupted. 'He's made me see it's about time I grew up. You see, even now you're worrying about me... Linda, now's a time you shouldn't have a care in the world.'

'Pregnancy isn't a condition that requires the switching off of all emotion,' chided Linda gently, relief replacing the fear which had filled her with that disjointed rush of words. 'And it doesn't alter the fact that you've been going through some pretty horrific experiences recently...and I don't only mean the collapse of your career—though, God knows, you've coped with that far better than most would have.'

And it might have crushed her, thought Jilly dazedly, had it not been overshadowed by something far more important to her.

'Linda...I'll get the coffee...you sit down.'

'No! Jilly, I'm not an invalid,' murmured Linda, giving her a gentle shove towards a chair—the chair on which, only moments before, Jean-Luc had sat, thought Jilly numbly as she sat down.

'When I'm the size of a mountain, perhaps I'll need you—but right now, you need me, Jilly.'

Jilly nodded, her silent admission of needing her sister frightening her with the confused welter of sensations it brought crowding into her mind.

'Jilly...I take it you told Jean-Luc why you'd been behaving as you had,' said Linda gently as she brought the coffee to the table.

Jilly nodded.

'Oh, Jilly, I warned you he'd take it badly,' she sighed, reaching out to take Jilly's tightly clenched hand. 'Darling, I'm the last person who'd advocate pampering the male ego, but...' She hesitated, then gave a small shrug. 'He came to the office one afternoon, when several models happened to be there. It was quite fascinating—seeing women's reaction to him...and his to them.'

'Linda, I'm not blind,' exclaimed Jilly bitterly. 'I know he's an exceptionally attractive man.'

'The point I was about to make, is that he's no womaniser...I'm not saying he's not perfectly aware of the effect he has on women—he is, and he's obviously had quite a bit of practice keeping them at arm's length... which is why, when he's placed in the unusual role of having to work at attracting, he's hardly likely to react well to his efforts being totally misread.'

'All right—so I offended his ego!' exclaimed Jilly impatiently. 'How was I supposed to know he found me physically attractive? He never stopped telling me how disgustingly skinny I was! He never stopped telling me how unspeakably childish he found me! What about my ego? It's all very well for Lady Lou to go on about the de Sauvignet men having a thing about honesty...'

'No man can ever be truly honest where his pride's at stake... or when he's being deeply hurt,' pointed out Linda quietly. 'Jilly, the way you were treating Jean-Luc... hell, if he'd been head over heels in love with you, he'd hardly have been likely to come out with it—straight-talking de Sauvignet or not!'

'Save your sympathy,' sighed Jilly. 'No hurt was inflicted on Jean-Luc by me... I merely dented his ego slightly.'

'I wonder,' murmured Linda sadly. 'I wish to God that's all that could be said for you.'

This time it was Jilly who took her sister's hand in a gesture of comfort.

'Serves me right for setting my sights so high,' she murmured, with a small laugh that didn't quite come off. 'After all... he was, to all intents and purposes, the man a computer decreed to be most people's idea of perfection.'

'Well... how did it go?' demanded Lady Louise, eagerness dancing on her features as she dragged Jilly through the partially opened door and closed it firmly behind her. 'Brr, it's cold... well?'

'It went a lot better than I'd expected,' Jilly replied, shedding her coat before following the old lady up the stairs. 'The biology was actually a doddle...and the others weren't too bad...hello, Charlie!'

'He's had his paws crossed for you all day, haven't you, my lad?' exclaimed Lady Louise excitedly. 'Now, tell me all about it...how the interviews went...and the French!'

'Why don't I nip down to the kitchen and make us a cuppa first?' murmured Jilly, her eyes twinkling mischievously.

'And why don't you stop tormenting a frail, defence-less old woman?' snorted Lady Louise impatiently.

Chuckling, Jilly gave her a placating hug.

'I could almost hear them wincing during the French oral,' she sighed. 'But at least they understood me, and I them...'

'You'll soon pick up the French when you're there,' interrupted Lady Louise impatiently. 'What about...'

'Lady Lou! *If*, not *when* I'm there,' protested Jilly. 'There were about twenty English applicants—and only places for five of them!'

'And how many of them would have been leading dancers, had it not been for a cruel twist of fate?'

'Most of them probably have some element of dancing in their backgrounds,' sighed Jilly, knowing her cautious words fell on deaf ears—as far as Lady Louise was concerned, there was no question of her failing.

But her chances of selection were no more than slightly above average, Jilly reminded herself. The ballet director had made that perfectly clear to her from the first day he had told her of the international foundation set up specifically to train specialists in modern techniques of diagnosing and treating the physical problems relating to dancers.

'Carry on with your intensive A-level course—you'll need a good background in those subjects to be selected. And should you not get in, you can carry on with your original plans,' he had advised her. 'They expect a smattering of conversational French—not that a lack of it would rule you out entirely.'

Jilly had immediately added French to her curriculum, while always keeping firmly in mind the director's cautions against too much optimism.

Lady Louise, however, found caution an alien concept. 'To be a student in Paris! Oh, Jilly, how I envy you,' had been her immediate reaction.

'Jilly, I hope you didn't sound as negative in your interviews as you do now,' fretted the old lady. 'They might think you weren't all that interested.'

'I made it very clear exactly how interested I am,' promised Jilly, an impish grin on her face as she turned to the cat. 'Charlie, do you ever get the feeling your ma can't wait to see the back of me?' she asked in a loud stage whisper.

'If he does, he could well be right,' retorted Lady Louise, rising. 'I think I'll take you up on that offer of tea. It's about time I got you your supper, my lad,' she added, turning to Charlie and picking him up.

'So, you really want to be rid of me, do you?' teased Jilly, following her down the stairs. 'You'd miss me, though, wouldn't you, Charlie?' she added to the cat, peering at her benignly from over his mistress's shoulder.

'No doubt he would,' chuckled Lady Louise, depositing him on the floor and opening the fridge door. 'Just as both he and I miss Jean-Luc...it's over four months since he's been here.'

Jilly picked up the kettle and filled it—all without missing a beat, a fact she found curiously consoling.

'Lady Lou, I'm not sure I follow your line of reasoning,' she stated quietly, horrified to hear the stark lifelessness now in her tone.

'Oh, I'm sure you do, darling,' contradicted Lady Louise firmly. 'For some reason, no doubt acceptable to the pair of you, it appears I'm not to be able to enjoy the presence of the two young people I love most in this world—not at the same time, at any rate.'

'Perhaps there's a good reason why he . . . why Jean-Luc hasn't been able to come over,' muttered Jilly, her eyes never leaving the teapot she was so meticulously tending to, though her heart had begun that stifling, once so familiar thudding.

When Lady Louise had returned from convalescing in France, her broaching of the subject of her grandson had been most uncharacteristically tentative. The unmistakable distress the mere mention of his name had caused Jilly had silenced her immediately. And it was a silence she had maintained, save a couple of obviously accidental lapses, until today.

'He should take a leaf out of your book—and do some growing up,' snapped Lady Louise. Then her expression softened. 'And it's almost as though you've been growing up before my eyes in these past months,' she added gently.

'Was I so terribly childish before?' asked Jilly miserably, all the old fears and uncertainties she'd hoped were behind her, now treacherously welling up in her . . . and all because of the mention of one man's name.

'You were a delight—but a child none the less. But what else could you have been, given that strange, almost claustrophobic little world that was your life . . . but the

day had to come when you would become an adult. Jilly,
don't you think that tea's stewed long enough?'

Her expression one of stark unhappiness, Jilly poured
the tea, then carried the two cups up to the living-room.

'I felt like a child straight from kindergarten in those
first few days at college,' admitted Jilly suddenly. 'I was
terrified . . . they seemed so . . . in awe of me almost. I put
it down to my being quite a few years older than the
others on my course . . . but it turned out that a couple
of the girls had seen me dance. They actually asked me
for my autograph!' She sat down, frowning as she picked
up her cup and took a hasty sip. 'They all seemed to
have this strange idea that a ballet dancer's life was one
of jet-setting sophistication . . . whereas I felt almost as
though I had just stepped out into the real world for the
first time. Lady Lou . . . this growing up you say I've done,
has it been for the better?' she finished hesitantly.

'On the whole, I think it has been,' murmured Lady
Louise gently. 'Nobody would ever have wished the way
it came about on you . . . one of my worst fears was that
the disintegration of your career might have embittered
you.' Her shrewd blue eyes met Jilly's as she finished
speaking.

'Why only on the whole, then?' asked Jilly quietly,
noticing those blue eyes flicker momentarily.

'Because somewhere along the line, a certain spark
has faded in you. A spark that had nothing to do with
how childlike or adult you might be—it was a vitality
that springs from the soul.' She hesitated, lifting her cup
and drinking from it before continuing, 'You faced up
to the loss of your career with a strength way beyond
your years . . . no, it wasn't that which dimmed that vital
spark in you,' she sighed, replacing her cup and levelling
her gaze with Jilly's. 'The day Jean-Luc brought you to

see me in the hospital, do you remember my speaking of the first time I met his father?'

Jilly nodded, a tense stillness creeping into her.

'I told you of my initial fears for Julia...because seeing you and Jean-Luc together brought me a feeling almost of *déjà vu*. Except that the tiny frisson of fear I felt for you seemed no more than an unwarranted reflex.' She paused, her eyes almost pleading as she seemed to wait for Jilly to respond. 'You, Jilly, I can read like a book...perhaps my interpretation of my grandson isn't so good.'

'Lady Lou...I'd give anything for this not to have rebounded on you, I know how much you love Jean-Luc...'

'If he's so small a man that he can't visit his grandmother because of guilt over...'

'It's not his guilt!' blurted out Jilly. 'It was all my fault...I got it into my head he was in love with Linda...and I don't blame you for looking at me like that,' she exclaimed, as her companion gave her a look that openly questioned her sanity. 'In the end I got caught up in the most complicated web of lies...'

'Fatal with a de Sauvignet,' sighed Lady Louise. 'I warned you.'

'I tried telling him the truth...or part of it, right after we left you,' whispered Jilly hoarsely. 'He returned to Paris a couple of days after.'

'You told him you'd thought he was in love with your sister?' Jilly nodded miserably.

'And that you loved him?'

'Of course not...how could I?' she choked. 'I'd only have added embarrassment to his anger...and anyway, it was only infatuation...I'd not have been normal if I hadn't fallen a little for a man as attractive and excit—

for a man like Jean-Luc,' she finished, her desperate attempt to convince herself turning her words almost to a plea.

'I'm pleased to hear it,' stated Lady Louise, with a sudden briskness. 'With your little infatuation for him behind you, you'll be able to see him when you get to Paris—and make your peace with him.' She beamed at Jilly in satisfaction. 'Why, you and he could travel back together during your holidays . . . I'm sure you'll end up the best of friends.'

'Lady Lou,' groaned Jilly, a glimmer of a smile reaching her lips despite the agonising turmoil reawakened in her, 'I hate to harp on such a minor point— but I haven't even been given a place on the course yet!'

CHAPTER TEN

'I KNOW it sounds corny—but I'm really beginning to understand why people always rabbit on about Paris in the spring!' The vivacious dark-haired girl, walking beside Jilly down the elegant tree-lined boulevard, flung back her head and gave a laugh of pure joy. 'Jilly, I just don't understand you—you've suddenly gone all subdued... what's got into you?'

'Now say all that in French,' chuckled Jilly, making a conscious effort to hang on to her rapidly waning spirit as she glanced affectionately at the girl with whom she now shared a room at the students' hostel.

'I'll tell you what your trouble is—you work too hard,' laughed Angela Morris—an ex-dancer like Jilly, whose career had been brought to a shattering halt by a road accident which, even two years later, had left her with a slight limp. 'It's Friday afternoon and we have a whole weekend of freedom from brain-racking before us... heck, Jilly, this friend of yours lives in a terribly posh area—who is he, for heaven's sake?'

Jilly felt her face muscles tighten, stilting her speech. 'He's the grandson of my next-door neighbour in England,' she muttered, the bravado with which she had casually asked Angela if she could accompany her part of the way to a nearby exhibition deserting her completely... her mind was in a state of sheer panic. She took a deep breath to steady herself. 'I promised her I'd visit him, but he's been away at some sort of seminar in South America for the past few weeks...'

'Oooh, how exotic—what does he do?'

'He's a mathematician,' stated Jilly, wondering if her voice sounded as strained to Angela as it did to her.

'*Très* heavy!' chuckled Angela, showing no signs of having noticed anything untoward. 'Thank God we don't need maths for this course, I'm useless at it. What time's he expecting you?'

'Actually, he's not,' replied Jilly, keeping her eyes firmly ahead of her. 'He probably won't be in...I thought I could leave a note...to show I'd at least made the effort.'

'Duty visits can be a bit heavy-going,' murmured Angela sympathetically. 'Wouldn't it have been better to ring him, though?'

'I tried—last night,' sighed Jilly. In fact, immediately after Lady Louise had phoned, she had dialled Jean-Luc's number so as not to give herself a chance to change her mind. 'With the help of a dictionary, I managed to report the fact that his phone's out of order. The operator was very understanding of my ghastly French— he even offered to give me private lessons.'

'Did he now?' giggled Angela, rolling her eyes. 'Is this his place?' she added, as Jilly suddenly halted by the drive to an imposingly elegant creeper-clad building. 'Wow, I bet those flats are a dream inside!' she exclaimed, then hesitated as she saw the tense strain on her friend's face. 'If you like, I could wait for you—or come in, even. The others won't mind if I'm a bit late,' she offered tentatively, her eyes now following Jilly's to the low-slung sports car that had turned past them and into the drive by which they stood.

As the car suddenly braked and halted half-way up the drive, Jilly could almost feel the colour draining from her face.

'Jilly?' murmured Angela, anxiety creeping into her tone.

Mustering every ounce of mental strength she possessed, Jilly turned to her companion and smiled reassuringly.

'I think that's him . . . now, off you go and enjoy the exhibition!'

'I suppose I ought to get a move on,' agreed Angela, her eyes widening slightly as they inspected the man stepping out of the car. 'God, the way you were talking, I expected a doddery old academic,' she whispered, grinning and giving a cheery wave as she set off. 'Good luck!'

She needed far more than good luck, thought Jilly numbly. For a start, she needed her brains examined for ever thinking she could cope with this, she told herself, panic mounting in her as the tall, dark-clad figure began walking slowly towards her.

Not one second of all those hours that had become days, weeks, then months, had altered the fact that she loved him, she realised, as she turned and began walking towards him. All that time telling herself she was cured . . . nothing had changed one iota of the love now recklessly crying out its existence in her.

She drew her lightweight coat more closely around her as she took those almost slow-motion steps that matched his, feeling a sudden chill despite the gentle warmth of the late afternoon sun gleaming through the air.

'Your phone . . . it's out of order,' she told him, as their steps independently drew to a wary halt, leaving several paces' width between them.

'So I believe . . . I can make outgoing calls, but not receive any.' His tone was formal, almost expressionless.

'I reported it. I...' She had almost to bite her tongue as she fought the childish urge to explain the rigmarole she had had in reporting it. 'They know it's not working.'

'Thank you. You're the third person who's told them—perhaps now they'll get around to fixing it.'

The oddly staccato formality of his words was like a lash against her ears. Why on earth had she listened to Lady Lou? What had possessed her to trick herself into thinking she could ever cope with this savage ache that came with seeing him again?

'I promised Lady Lou...ise I'd come to see you,' she informed him stiltedly. And having done so, you might as well go, taunted an angry voice inside her. Far from welcoming her, the man was having difficulty in being civil towards her.

'Jilly, I...look, would you mind if I parked the car? I'm blocking the drive.'

'I didn't mean to keep you,' she blurted out, sensing a means of escape and frantically clutching at it. 'I'd better go...all I wanted was to keep my promise to your grandmother...' She broke off as he reached her side and, catching her lightly by the arm, began leading her towards the car.

'I'm sure her intention wasn't for it to be as literal as that—to see me and go.' There was the merest trace of amusement in his tone, though Jilly's eyes refused to look up into his face, they remained firmly fixed on the door he was opening. 'In you get.'

It took them all of five seconds to reach the car spaces to the side of the building, and it was in total silence that he led her inside and across a richly carpeted foyer and to the foot of a huge marbled staircase.

'We could use the lift, if you'd prefer—I'm on the second floor.'

'No...I prefer to walk,' replied Jilly stiltedly, her mind jarred by memories of the laughter they had once shared now calling out to her like fading ghosts.

This was a million times worse than anything she could ever have imagined, she told herself hopelessly, as she followed him up the stairs. Was it really only last night that she had actually envisaged herself exchanging light-hearted pleasantries with him...confounding him with her relaxed and new-found sophistication? Now all she could think of was the bliss that would be her escape.

Her immediate impression of the flat into which he led her was of a stark spaciousness that was curiously peaceful. The room into which he ushered her strengthened that impression. It was large and high-ceilinged, with the stark beauty of its line accentuated by the almost minimal presence of furniture. Apart from several huge oriental cushions, and a large, very low, blackwood table, there was scarcely any furniture to speak of.

'It's beautiful!' exclaimed Jilly, so spontaneously the words were out before she was aware of them.

'You surprise me,' he murmured. 'I usually see a mental shopping list gleaming in the eyes of most women when they first see this place.' He gave a small shrug. 'I can't stand the clutter of furniture...give me your coat.'

Her movements almost robotic, Jilly slipped out of her coat and handed it to him.

'Would you prefer tea, or coffee?' he asked, with the polite formality of a diligent host.

'Coffee, thank you,' replied Jilly, moving towards a very large, low-silled window, one of three overlooking the boulevard.

Time did allow one to forget, she told herself despairingly. She had forgotten the memories that just the sight of his hands reaching for her coat could revive. Of those hands exploring her body, learning its secrets while they imparted their own with the heady magic of their touch.

Think about something else...the weather, exhorted a frantic inner voice. Think of your course, your future! You've come such a long way in these past few months...hang on to what you have, to what you've made of yourself!

'Jilly?'

'That was quick,' she murmured, gaining strength from the calm in those words as she moved to one of the large cushions and sank down on it, tucking her legs beneath her as she watched him place a tray on the table. 'I understand now why the table is so low.'

His eyes rose to hers, a trick of the light seeming to make them dance against hers with an intimacy that left her breathless from the frantic somersaulting of her stomach.

'It's Japanese...is that enough milk?'

Jilly nodded, though her eyes had never checked, caught by the almost imperceptible tremor in the hand that held out the cup to her.

'So—what brings you to Paris, Jilly?'

Her eyes widened in puzzlement as he sat down beside her, his long legs crossing with athletic ease into an almost classical yoga position.

'Didn't Lady Lou tell you?' she asked.

'My grandmother's not speaking to me...a point she rings me at every available opportunity to remind me of,' he murmured. 'She's even resorted to withholding information about Charlie!' As he finished speaking, he gave a soft, throaty chuckle.

Jilly was conscious of her own sharp intake of breath as that laughter seemed to ripple like a warm caress across her senses. It was a sound she had been starved of for all these months, she realised helplessly... a sound she had ached for even while refusing to acknowledge the ache within her.

'He had a set-to with a dog which moved in across the green, just before I left. Charlie wasn't hurt, though.'

'But did the dog survive?' chuckled Jean-Luc.

'Just. Lady Lou tells me he and Charlie have come to an understanding that almost amounts to friendship.'

'Tells you?' His eyebrows rose in that familiar questioning way of theirs. 'Jilly, how long have you been away? You haven't told me what you're doing in Paris.'

'I got sidetracked,' she smiled, then told him.

Half-way through what she was saying, he moved, uncurling his long body and stretching it out, his chin resting on his hand as he gazed up at her.

'You know, Jilly, you'd have every right to feel very proud of yourself,' he told her gently, then added in slow, clear French. 'How long does your course last?'

'Well, it's a one-year intensive course, but...'

'In French,' he chided softly.

'But my French doesn't cover being able to say that we'll virtually be their students for the rest of our working lives. As more is learned about dancers' problems—and ways of treating them are devised—so the knowledge will be passed on to us. Jean-Luc, it's so exciting to be in practically in at the start of something as vital as this. It's so international—we have several Russian students on the course—and it's something the ballet world has cried out for.'

'Something you cried out for, Jilly,' he stated in a strangely hollow voice.

'None of this could have helped me. You see, nothing can change the fact that my body just isn't capable of coping with the physical punishment of a dancing career.' As she spoke, Jilly found her hands clenching tightly, fighting an almost overwhelming need to reach out and touch the dark head so near her. 'But perhaps the day will come when embryo dancers with my type of build will be spotted and deterred before embarking on years of waste.'

'And you see yours as wasted years?' he asked.

Jilly looked down at him, startled by the sorrow in his tone.

'It would be dishonest of me not to admit to some residual bitterness... it's only in these months since I've stopped dancing that I've really begun to see the amount of pain my body had learned to accept as normal.' She gave a small, dismissive shrug. 'But without those years there wouldn't be this new life opening up for me... the students on the course without much dancing in their backgrounds are real brain-boxes... I'd never have stood a chance without those years of training behind me.'

'Considering what your brain appears to have soaked up so easily since we last met, I'd say it had every right to be classed as a box... if you get my meaning.'

With another of those chuckles that wrought havoc with her senses, he leapt to his feet and made his way towards the far end of the room. On each side of a huge, marbled fireplace were bookcases reaching high up the wall. He dropped to his haunches to examine the lower left-hand shelves that contained, not books but row upon row of videos.

'This came while I was away,' he announced, selecting a video and returning with it to sit by her, 'the only indication that it's from my grandmother being the fact that it was something she once told me I should see...do you remember?'

He dropped the video into her lap. Jilly picked it up, a strange, unsettling feeling fluttering through her as she glanced down at the four people depicted on the cover—two of them herself and Justin Malenka.

'Yes—the film of *Don Quixote*,' she whispered hoarsely. It was the ballet in which she and Justin had achieved international recognition almost overnight—her first and last major role.

'I arrived back yesterday afternoon,' stated Jean-Luc in a curiously hesitant voice. 'I watched it five times last night...actually five and a half...I think I must have fallen asleep in the dream scene on the sixth viewing.'

'But why?' croaked Jilly. 'I mean...what made you watch it all those times? Did it turn you into a ballet fan all of a sudden?'

'I watched it all those times, because...Jilly, I never understood!' he exclaimed suddenly. 'Dear God, when I think of my unforgivable arrogance!'

'Jean-Luc, I don't quite follow you,' Jilly protested, her eyes widening in puzzlement as he leapt angrily to his feet and strode to the middle window, gazing moodily down through it.

'My grandmother tried explaining to me...that I couldn't possibly know, or even begin to understand what you were going through...unless, perhaps, I had seen you dance.'

'Why should you be expected to understand? At least you tried to help me...'

'And wasn't that big of me?' he exclaimed harshly. 'I actually deigned to go along to a couple of your classes to put myself in the picture. My—weren't you lucky to have me to distract you from your little problem!'

'Jean-Luc, please...stop this,' begged Jilly, recoiling from the harsh, self-mocking words ringing in her ears. Any moment now he was going to tell her just how far he had been prepared to go in his self-imposed task of distracting her...just how far he had gone.

'Why do you want me to stop, Jilly?' he demanded accusingly. 'At least allow me the luxury of voicing my shame!'

'For heaven's sake, Jean-Luc!' she exclaimed, desperate to silence those angry words for fear of what they would bring. 'There's no need for you to feel shame...you know no more about ballet than I do about...about mathematics. I didn't expect you to understand.'

'No...in fact you expected nothing of me, Jilly,' he stated hoarsely, returning to her and dropping to his haunches before her. 'Yet I expected...demanded...so much of you.'

Wordlessly, Jilly shook her head. She needed to move away—to escape the unsettling darkness in those eyes now holding her prisoner in the intensity of their hypnotic gaze.

'Jilly, I should never have made love to you...'

'No!' she protested, her hands tight against her ears as she leapt to her feet in frantic desperation.

'What do you mean—no?' he exploded, rising to tower over her. 'Why the hell did you come here if you're not prepared even to talk?'

'I told you...I came because I promised your grandmother I would. And now I want to go!'

'What have you against hearing the truth, Jilly?' he demanded harshly.

'Because it hurts—that's why!' she almost screamed at him, all the explosive tension bottled up inside her finding release in those words as the fragile dam within her burst. 'It's not only the de Sauvignets who need truth...you're not unique! It's what most of us want...need. Not the terrible complications and distortions that come from lies.' She could hear the raggedness in her breaking voice, but she was powerless to stem her flow of anguished words...she had to keep filling the silence because of her overwhelming dread of the words he might speak. 'But there must be times when even those paragons of honesty, the de Sauvignets, find themselves having to disguise truths too painful to face...or don't they feel? Perhaps they don't hurt in the way we mortals do.'

'Jilly, for God's sake...what's all this rubbish about the de Sauvignets?' he asked hoarsely, bewilderment etched on his features.

'Lady Lou...'

'*Nom de Dieu*, there are times I could happily throttle my grandmother!' he exclaimed angrily.

'Leave her out of this,' retaliated Jilly protectively. 'All she said was that the de Sauvignet men were renowned for...I don't know...having a thing about complete honesty.'

'I've never heard such rubbish,' he groaned in disbelief. 'We tell as many lies as the next man—God knows, I've had to recently!'

'But you don't make any allowance for others deceiving *you*!' countered Jilly heatedly. 'Or have you forgotten your performance over my lying to you?' Suddenly the anger died in her, leaving her empty and spent. 'Jean-Luc...there's no point in any of this. Please...just get me my coat.'

'All right, Jilly, I'll get you your coat,' he muttered tonelessly, moving away towards the door. Then he half turned, leaning his head against the jamb. 'Hell, you understood me so little, you even thought I'd had a hand in your losing that role...'

'No! No,' she protested hoarsely. 'I was worried when you told me about the trust...but in my heart of hearts I knew losing the role had nothing to do with you. I had no right to vent my disappointment on you...which is what I did.'

'Jilly, can't you see...how talking can go some way to clearing all these misunderstandings?' he asked wearily. 'And something tells me how wrong I was not to talk to you...that I owe it to you to swallow what now strikes me as my inordinate pride. How could two people be so different?' He groaned suddenly. 'Me with my over-abundance of self-confidence, you with no awareness of—let alone confidence in—your intellect and beauty? Why, Jilly?'

'That's something I've only really begun to understand very recently,' whispered Jilly, something almost compelling her to answer that soft, yet chillingly expressionless chant of words. 'For almost as long as I can remember, my life has been a constant battle with my body...the pain...the need always to keep my weight down. In a way, I was at war with my body. It's not possible to have confidence in—or think of in terms of beauty—something you regard only as an enemy.'

'Yet instead of my instilling you with the confidence you merited, you began undermining mine.'

Jilly felt herself start at those softly sighed words, then immediately began trying to convince herself she had misheard them.

'Until you, my self-confidence was an unquestioned totality. Yet you, Jilly, introduced me to a dark side of my ego I had never known existed.' He gave a bitter laugh. 'Unlike my grandmother, I can't speak for de Sauvignet men in general, but you were right in that this de Sauvignet man found himself with a truth he couldn't face . . . for no other reason than sparing his ego.'

Jilly gave a small shake of her head, as though trying to shake free from a trance.

'You see, Jilly, though I demanded honesty from you, I gave you none in return.' He straightened suddenly. 'It was the fragility of my ego that allowed me to make love to you, while forbidding me to tell you how much I loved you.'

Jilly felt her legs tense to support her as his words hit her with all the force of a physical attack, and the few seconds—if that—which it took for the meaning of those words to become clear in the chaos of her mind, seemed like an eternity; an impression only strengthened in her reeling thoughts by his disappearance from the doorway.

'Jean-Luc, please!' she cried out. 'Please . . . you can't run away.'

'I'm not running away,' he informed her coldly, reappearing in the doorway and scowling blackly across the room at her. 'You asked for your coat—I'm getting it.'

'I don't want my coat,' she managed, her words a breathless battle against the cacophony of confusion that was her mind.

She hadn't imagined his words, insisted an almost desperate voice inside her, as she remained as though rooted where she stood, her still uncertain eyes pleading with that scowling face to tell her she hadn't imagined those words.

'Jean-Luc...I'm trying to move...my legs won't obey,' she pleaded, her arms reaching out helplessly as a wild, suffocating joy ran loose in her, trapped within the rigid confines of her uncooperating body.

In a couple of alarmed strides, he was beside her, his face pale with anxiety.

'Jilly, what's wrong, for God's sake? I thought this was all behind you ...'

'Jean-Luc, please ... put your arms round me,' she whispered.

It was the expression of undisguised suspicion creeping through the fear on his handsome features that added sudden doubts to the riot of emotions devastating her as he stepped nearer and gingerly placed wooden arms around her body.

She hadn't imagined his words, she protested silently, her body, as though freed by his cautious touch, now swaying towards his. And it was his soft groan, the tremor rippling through arms shedding their caution to tighten fiercely around her, that told her she had imagined nothing.

'How could you be so stupid?' she chided huskily, while her arms clung possessively. 'Not to see how much I loved you ... how I'll always love you.'

'Oh, Jilly,' he groaned, his lips whispering soft, incoherent words as they sought hers, opening in a bruising impatience that was almost anger as they found what they sought.

Then he was lifting her, holding her against him, his mouth locked in passionate plunder with hers as he lowered her down to the cushions.

'Jean-Luc ...'

'No...don't say anything,' he begged hoarsely, his words those of a man fighting against the grip of a trance. 'Just let me hold you in my arms...let me drown in your arms...let me trap this moment for ever before it slips from me,' he begged disjointedly.

Then his hands were moving against her body, searching and caressing, as though needing the comfort of touch to confirm a reality his mind had yet to accept.

As her hands instinctively followed the lead of his, needing every bit as much of the confirmation his sought, a long sigh shuddered through him that seemed to gentle the frantic fierceness possessing him.

'Oh, Jilly, how I love you,' he whispered, his words soft and dazed. 'Nothing matters but you...you're all in life that matters to me!'

His hair was a silky softness brushing against her neck as his head lowered to rest against her breasts.

'Jean-Luc, I love you...I can't bring myself to believe this is happening,' she choked, her trembling fingers entwining in his hair as his face burrowed hard against her. 'All I know is that I love you...I love you.'

He raised his head, the eyes that gazed into hers now filled with the soft darkness of languor.

'Oh, my sweet, loving Jilly,' he whispered huskily, his fingers caressing gently in her hair. 'For a moment, there was complete chaos in my mind...the only reasonably sane thought in it was that our bodies should become one in love once again.' He shook his head, a half-smile forming on his lips. 'Not that the temptation isn't still strongly there, as my body is so blatantly proclaiming...not to mention yours,' he added with a throaty shiver of laughter, as his head lowered once more for his lips to tease provocatively against the pulse beating a wild tattoo at her throat. 'But I know now that when we next make love, it must be without those unspoken, unanswered doubts still lingering between us. Never as before... when there was so much uncertainty, so much conflict raging in my heart,' he whispered sadly. 'That first time... I was torn by the terrible paradox of not being able to accept I was the first, bludgeoning my mind against all my instincts because I couldn't bear to believe I might merely be serving a purpose...'

'Jean-Luc, how could you possibly have believed those terrible things I said about wanting to shed my virginity?' she groaned, her arms cradling the head again nestling against her, desperate to protect him from the pain her own foolish pride had inflicted on him. 'No woman in her right mind would even think, let alone admit to something like that.'

'But a man no longer in his right mind couldn't be blamed for believing it,' he sighed, his fingers reaching up to stroke her cheek. 'Especially a man who felt as though he'd been walking round with a placard slung round his neck, proclaiming his love for you...'

'I beg your pardon!' murmured Jilly, soft indignation in her tone, despite the melting surge of love those exaggerated words had churned up in her.

'How else could my behaviour be described?' he demanded, his indignation far more forceful than hers. 'There I was, with more than enough in the way of worry on my plate—at my grandmother's bedside often until the small hours, and becoming increasingly anxious about the state of her health. And what did I do? I added you to my worries... not that I had any choice. Jilly, only a man who's falling headlong into love—even if he isn't aware of it—goes racing around London the way I did—quizzing specialists on a case he knows next to nothing about.'

'They probably thought you were mad,' murmured Jilly contentedly, her cheek rubbing against the silky darkness of his hair.

'The first one certainly did,' he admitted, with no discernible trace of embarrassment. 'I made the mistake of telling him the truth—that you were a virtual stranger. I think he took me for some sort of crank... he had me out of his consulting-rooms with disconcerting speed.'

'Poor Jean-Luc,' murmured Jilly, choking back laughter.

'Poor Jean-Luc nothing!' he retorted. 'I learn quickly... that's when I started dragging poor Linda around with me... when she couldn't make it, I told them you were my mistress...'

'Why mistress, for heaven's sake?' gasped Jilly, her laughter bursting free.

'Because a husband would be entitled to a darn sight more information than I had... from the specialists you were already seeing,' he exclaimed impatiently. 'Anyway, that's what I told them. And, after all that... you had the gall to turn round and inform me you thought I was in love with your sister!'

His head rose and, though his words had been tinged with exasperated humour, there was the bitterness of remembered pain in the eyes gazing down at her. 'Jilly, when you came out with that—I was convinced I'd squandered my love on a raving nutcase!'

'Perhaps that's just what I'd turned into,' sighed Jilly sadly. 'I was experiencing jealousy for the first time in my life... and it was destroying my reason. Even after I knew why you and Linda had spent so much time together... even knowing the secrecy had been to protect me... that terrible jealousy wouldn't leave me. It was as though I had to convince myself you loved Linda, because my complete lack of self-confidence refused to let me contemplate that you could love me.'

'Jealousy—that's something I became expert in over-night, and something I never wish to experience again,' he said with a shudder of disgust. 'I almost had to resort to breaking my own fingers just to keep them from Justin's throat. Just as I had a similar problem keeping them from your throat when you twisted that final knife in to me... Jilly, I don't know which tormented me more—the thought of you making love to me because you were trying to save your sister, or...'

'I saw those terrible lies as my only alternative to the truth—that my body had given you all the love I pos-sessed... all the love my heart couldn't dare dream you might return,' she murmured, her hands reaching up to caress his face, as though to smooth away the bitterness of memory from it—wanting to see mirrored in it the riotous happiness racing through every part of her. 'Jean-Luc, I love you... *je t'aime.*'

'Words,' he muttered dismissively, his arms tight-ening around her as a lazy smile softened the bitterness from his features. 'I'll need a great deal more than mere words before I'm fully convinced of all this love you claim for me. My God, this eloquence of yours almost has me convinced it's something approaching the awesome magnitude of mine!'

She gave a small shiver of contentment as her hands cupped his face, her body melting against his in soft se-duction as she tried to draw his head down to her lips.

'Jean-Luc, I give you everything,' she murmured huskily. 'I have to, because my love is all of me, and all of my love is yours.'

'Still mere words,' he taunted softly, his head resisting the pull of her hands as his lips teased against her mouth.

'Tell me what you want, and it's yours,' she whispered.

'You're too reckless, my Jilly. I could ask you to end that new career you've just found...ask you to turn your back on it just for me.'

'If you asked that...I...I could only do it,' she replied, her heart fiercely denying the small black cloud looming darkly on the horizon of her happiness.

'Jilly, no man who loved you would ever ask that of you,' he chided softly. 'The only demand I intend making of you is that you marry me—the soonest moment we possibly can. Jilly, my darling, please don't cry!' he begged, his lips frantic as they moved from one to the other of her cheeks to kiss away the huge tears suddenly spilling down them. 'It was that demon ego of mine having a last evil fling bringing your career into question,' he protested fervently. 'Jilly, all I want is to be able to show you how I love you! I'll carry your books to classes for you, if you want...I'll do the cooking for us! Jilly...Jilly, you're laughing!' he exclaimed in sudden indignation.

'Of course I'm laughing, my beautiful idiot! Haven't you ever heard of tears of happiness? Pure, unadulterated, unbelievable happiness!' she cried, her arms clinging to him with the fierce delight of love.

'Does that by any chance mean you'll marry me?'

'As soon as we possibly can—sooner even!' she vowed, clinging even harder to him as her mind examined the expression 'bursting with happiness' and wondering, with a twinge of anxiety, if this wasn't what was happening to her.

'Jilly,' he croaked. 'I can't breathe!'

She loosened her ecstatic arms a fraction.

'Did you actually say you'd marry me?' he panted theatrically. 'What with my brain suffering from oxygen starvation, I'm having difficulty hearing.'

'I did,' she chuckled contentedly. 'But I was thinking...perhaps I ought to sample a few menus before I subject myself to a lifetime of your cooking.'

'I didn't mean to imply a lifetime of it. In fact, I was thinking more along the lines of a week at the most...then I could get someone in to...Jilly!' he groaned suddenly. 'Could we dispense with these happy tears? I'm beginning to feel a bit soggy!'

'I've nearly run dry,' she promised tremulously, gazing up into his laughter-filled eyes. 'It's just hearing you talk about us...about a future together...I can't describe how it makes me feel.'

'Jilly, for me there is no future unless it holds you,' he told her huskily, a sultry darkness in his eyes as his lips met hers.

At first there was a gentle sweetness in the soft exploration of their mouths. Then passion was a sudden white-hot need, melting their bodies in its desperate hunger.

'Go away,' he groaned, pushing her from him, only to drag her fiercely back into his arms. 'Jilly, there are things we must see to.'

'What things?' she asked dazedly, as he drew her upright.

'For a start, we must ring my grandmother...I have this vivid mental picture of her loitering by the phone, waiting for precisely the news we'll give her. Something tells me she's engineered all this—and I adore her all the more for having done so.'

'I can't wait to tell her,' sighed Jilly blissfully, her fingers entwining contentedly in his as he drew her to her feet.

'Then we'll ring Linda...and then we'll go and collect your things. Jilly, you will be allowed to move in with me...you will want to?' he asked, his words suddenly uncertain.

'Yes, and yes,' she murmured, her cheek pressing against his arm. 'Jean-Luc, I've just thought! We'll have to break the news gently to Linda...the baby's due any day and the surprise could be too much for her.'

'I dare say she'll thank us for getting things going. And I very much doubt if our news will come as that much of a shock to her anyway,' he chuckled, then added softly. 'And don't worry—we shan't be starting a family until you're completely ready.'

'Which is right now,' she whispered huskily. 'That's the only black mark against this course I'm on...that it means having to wait to have your baby, Jean-Luc...but only for a short while; it's an ideal career for a working mother.'

'And you'll have no problems working with a ballet company here in Paris,' he told her softly, pulling her closer. 'I'll have you fluent in French in next to no time.' He grinned, then kissed the end of her nose. 'Though there are a couple more black marks against this course of yours. Charlie's ma won't hear of us getting married anywhere but in England...so that means a frantic flying visit next weekend. I hope my family can make it at such short notice...they're all going to adore you just as I...'

'Jean-Luc, are you saying we can get married next weekend?' croaked Jilly, through a delirium of pure joy.

'I am. But your course—and, to be honest, my commitments, too—will mean no honeymoon.' He turned and took her fully into his arms. 'Except that I plan turning the rest of our lives into our honeymoon,' he whispered huskily, his lips moving seductively against her throat.

'Jean-Luc,' she pleaded, as his lips sent shivers of excited longing shooting through her. 'You're beginning to make me feel the way I felt when you told me to go away because you had more important things to see to,' she babbled slightly incoherently.

'I couldn't possibly have told you to go away,' he murmured distractedly.

'But you did,' gasped Jilly, what little resolution she possessed weakening rapidly.

'OK, my little bully,' he answered with a breathless chuckle, spinning her out of his arms. 'We'll use the phone in the hall...unless you'd prefer we used the one in the bedroom.' Laughing, he slipped his arm around her as they made their way to the hall. 'And if my grandmother starts offering to find us a Charlie replica as a wedding present, promise me you'll dissuade her...it will be a long time before my ego recovers from the battering it took competing with that wretched cat...forgive me,' he chuckled, picking up the receiver and gazing down at her from laughter-filled eyes. 'I can't think what came over me! What I meant to say was that utterly delightful...hell, Jilly,' he groaned, rolling his eyes theatrically as he began dialling. 'What if she insists on bringing him to our wedding? Hello, *Grand-mère*...' He gave a sudden roar of delight and passed Jilly the receiver, hugging her to him as she took it. 'She's demanding to speak to her future granddaughter-in-law!'

Harlequin Presents®

Coming Next Month

Available in April wherever paperback books are sold, or through
Harlequin Reader Service·

In the U.S.
901 Fuhrmann Blvd.
P O Box 1397
Buffalo, N.Y 14240-1397

In Canada
P O Box 603
Fort Erie, Ontario
L2A 5X3

You'll flip . . . your pages won't!
Read paperbacks *hands-free* with

Book Mate · I

The perfect "mate" for all your romance paperbacks

Traveling • Vacationing • At Work • In Bed • Studying • Cooking • Eating

Perfect size for all standard paperbacks, this wonderful invention makes reading a pure pleasure! Ingenious design holds paperback books OPEN and FLAT so even wind can't ruffle pages— leaves your hands free to do other things. Reinforced, wipe-clean vinyl-covered holder flexes to let you turn pages without undoing the strap . . . supports paperbacks so well, they have the strength of hardcovers!

Pages turn WITHOUT opening the strap

SEE-THROUGH STRAP

Reinforced back stays flat

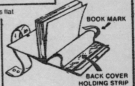

Built in bookmark

BOOK MARK

BACK COVER HOLDING STRIP

10 x 7¼ opened
Snaps closed for easy carrying, too

Harlequin Superromance®

LET THE GOOD TIMES ROLL . . .

Add some Cajun spice to liven up your New Year's celebrations and join Superromance for a romantic tour of the rich Acadian marshlands and the legendary Louisiana bayous.

CAJUN MELODIES, starting in January 1990, is a three-book tribute to the fun-loving people who've enriched America by introducing us to crawfish étouffé and gumbo, zydeco music and the Saturday night party, the *fais-dodo*. And learn about loving, Cajun-style, as you meet the tall, dark, handsome men who win their ladies' hearts with a beautiful, haunting melody. . . .

Book One: *Julianne's Song*, January 1990
Book Two: *Catherine's Song*, February 1990
Book Three: *Jessica's Song*, March 1990